By the Rivers of Babylon

ANTÓNIO LOBO ANTUNES

By the Rivers
of Babylon

Translated from the Portuguese by
Margaret Jull Costa

A MARGELLOS
WORLD REPUBLIC OF LETTERS BOOK

Yale UNIVERSITY PRESS | NEW HAVEN & LONDON

English translation copyright © 2023 by Margaret Jull Costa. Originally published as *Sôbolos Rios Que Vão* © António Lobo Antunes, 2010.

Yale University Press books may be purchased in quantity for educational, business, or promotional use. For information, please e-mail sales.press@yale.edu (U.S. office) or sales@yaleup.co.uk (U.K. office).

Set in Source Serif type by Motto Publishing Services.
Printed in the United States of America.

Library of Congress Control Number: 2022940592
ISBN 978-0-300-23341-4 (hardcover : alk. paper)

A catalogue record for this book is available from the British Library.

This paper meets the requirements of ANSI/NISO Z39.48-1992 (Permanence of Paper).

10 9 8 7 6 5 4 3 2 1

For Tereza and especially for Rui
—António

By the Rivers of Babylon

21 March 2007

From the hospital window in Lisbon it wasn't the people arriving or the cars parked among the trees or an ambulance that he saw, it was the pine trees, then the train, houses, more pine trees and the mountains in the background distanced from him by the mist, it was the bird of his fear with no branch to perch on, the tips of its wings trembling, the prickly chestnut from the tree that used to stand at the entrance to the garden and that was now inside him, silently growing, what the doctor called cancer, as soon as the doctor called it cancer the church bells began tolling and a cortege headed off to the cemetery with an open coffin and a child inside, other children dressed as seraphim guarding the coffin, people, or rather only the sound of their boots and therefore not people, just boots and more boots, when his grandmother sitting on the wall beside him stopped crossing herself, he became aware of the smell of jam in the pantry, pots of jam on every step, and as with those intact jam jars nothing happened, lying on the gurney after the examination, he very nearly said to the doctor

—Nothing happened, right?

and no, nothing happened, because the jars were intact, his grandmother who had died so many years ago was there beside him alive, his late grandfather who had died even longer ago was there too with his hearing aid, reading the newspaper, his grandfather's silence alarmed him and made the prickly chestnut in his guts dilate, scratch, ache, I place it on a granite slab, I strike it with my hammer and squash the disease flat, someone he couldn't see was pushing him and the gurney down the corridor, he was aware of the rain, of faces, signs, the curate's housekeeper standing on the porch while he was thinking

—It's my coffin they're pushing along

offering him some grapes

—Would you like some grapes, dear?

then immediately vanishing, it bothered him not being able to remember the housekeeper's name, he could remember her apron, her slippers, her laugh, but not her name, and because he couldn't remember her name he wouldn't get better, on the sofa his grandfather folded up his newspaper and didn't even look at him, he felt like asking

—Is there nothing you can do for me?

and the most he could hope for was his grandfather's hand cupping his ear

—What?

his brow furrowed and directed at no one

—What did he say?

and so the bird of his fear continued to fly around in circles, those are the roots of his feet and his fingers clutching the sheet, poor things, the people waiting for the elevator allowed the gurney in first, they glanced at him for a moment, then forgot him, how could they possibly forget him, during the grape harvest his grandmother would give him a straw hat with a worn-out elastic strap to wear, why do elastic straps always wear out and why do most cups have chipped handles, he was six, maybe seven, he would find mica pebbles and turn them this way and that so that they caught the light, he couldn't believe none of those people had ever spotted him on the balcony facing the mountains as he tried to trap the insects living in the creeper in an empty matchbox, not that he ever caught any, he wasn't in the hospital in March in the rain, he was in the village in August, if they sent him off on an errand, he would change sidewalks before he reached the house where Dona Lucrécia was sitting in her invalid's chair at the top of the steps, waving her stick at him

—Come here, boy

and there he was with no one to protect him just as there was no one to protect him now, Dona Lucrécia waiting in the same ward where he was being taken, he decided to tell the nurse

—Discharge Dona Lucrécia first

and when he repeated this

—Discharge Dona Lucrécia first

he could have sworn that a hand cupped one ear

—What?

and the newspaper arriving at midday, goodness how everything repeats itself, everything until now that is, apart from the hospital and the illness, whenever his grandfather put his glasses away in his pocket one or two fingers would inevitably get caught in the lining, along with his spectacles, Dona Lucrécia's stick

—Come here, boy

and the ferocity of those endlessly chewing cheeks, this corridor smells of the pharmacy in the village, where, the story goes, wolves would appear outside the school in winter, you could see their tracks on the ground and the mauled remains of a calf, just like his remains after surgery tomorrow, a female medical student peered round the door just as his mother always did before turning out the light

—Go to sleep now

with the light on she was his mother, without it just a dark silhouette, steps that disappeared off into the thousand rooms of the house, no not steps but pearls on a necklace when the string breaks, the number of creatures, people, his mother became as she walked away, and not one of them stayed to help save him from the night, the smell of jam in the pantry returned and vanished, and he fell into the folly of issuing an order

—Stay with me, smell

leaving him feeling more alone and more afraid, what a strange diagnosis they had given him, cancer, how unthinkable to die and the sound of boots and more boots in the village and a dog stopping to look, it may not have known what was happening to him but its nose would know, dogs can sense misfortunes, they sit back on their haunches and stretch out their necks and howl, his grandmother

—I just hope the shoe mender doesn't drink so much that he can't ring the church bell

and when the bell rings out, the pigeons take fright and fly off to the derelict chapel, returning in the afternoon to settle on top of the Town Hall, they're easily startled, a pine cone falling, the creaking of cartwheels, a mule stopping suddenly, teeth bared, sobbing and sobbing, his grandfather, looking around him suspiciously, hears something or other without understanding what it can be, namely, I'll operate tomorrow, he never spoke, if he realized people were talking about him, he would smile, try and smile like your grandfather, it isn't a smile, it's an expression of apology or humble agreement, when he fed you, he would hold out the spoon, forming an O with his own mouth, then he would wipe your mouth with his handkerchief but always miss the crumbs, and start again

—Just another two and a half spoonfuls

on the balcony looking out at the mountains and the tranquil chestnut trees, the tranquil cups and saucers, almost everything in his childhood was tranquil except the pump sucking mud out of the well, the rustle of the corn, and the madman with a blanket round his shoulders announcing to the goats

—The whole world is mine, you wretches, not a star moves without my saying so

and him in the hospital not speaking, why bother, the madman knew what was what

—Fix this for me, Senhor Borges

and in the living room above, someone was stamping, enjoying himself, punctuating his sentences, Senhor Borges disappeared round the hedge and the beech trees swallowed him up, anxiety placed a claw about his heart made of fear and tears, difficult to regulate in secret, not a sound even though everything inside him was screaming, every unmade gesture was screaming, every movement of his head was screaming, every inch of skin on the sheet was screaming, if the stamping stopped for a moment they would hear

—What's wrong with the little fellow?

what's wrong are the rotten cells in his intestines invading him and destroying lungs, bones, liver, and the children dressed as seraphim with their wings clumsily attached to their backs, what a terrible thing death is and how comical, mocking you, despising you, in the History book the dates when the kings were born and died were a matter of indifference to him because they weren't his dates, the bishop closed the eyelids of King João II, and King João II

—Not yet

his great-grandparents in the photo album

—Not yet

as well as the man with the moustache, the bald one, the one in the colonel's uniform with all the medals, just turn the page and

—Not yet

a faded fellow who refused to hear, his heart missing a beat without his realizing because his cheeks were wet with tears, when the brown ox died they had to break its legs so that it would fit in the hole, its eyelids still visibly eyelids despite being covered in flies

—Not yet

and we didn't care about his suffering or his wet cheeks, he recalled the sound of the earth on the drum of the ox's back, a worm made into two worms by the mattock and the two greedily eating each other, and the lizard learning to be a stone in a crack in the wall and then his father playing tennis at the hotel with the Englishmen who owned the tungsten mine and him running to pick up the balls that jumped over the fence, he picked up the last one by the swimming pool, where a blonde foreigner was drying herself, and the ball stayed clutched to his chest, he too learning to be a stone, in a moment of exaltation he did not then understand.

—What's this?

wishing he was a grown man, timidity, embarrassment, if the blonde foreigner smiled at him he would kneel down or run away, how mysterious life is, they used to bathe him in a tub in the kitchen and how awkward he felt at appearing naked before the maid, small, skinny, submissive, as he was now there in the ward, once again small, skinny and submissive, the blonde foreigner went back into the hotel carrying a little basket of sun creams, and each buttock was an amphora that filled up with him, then emptied him out without taking him with her, he didn't return the ball to his father, because it wasn't a ball, it was his blood beating fast, even today his blood beats fast when he remembers her, he kept the ball in a chest of drawers and now and then stroked it with a delicacy never repeated in all these years, from the hospital window he can see fewer people now and fewer cars, soon it will be night and his wretched body lying in the darkness, his voice independently of him

—No

and for how many weeks would he still have a voice, for how many weeks

—No

until his throat also rotted, and when his throat had completely rotted away there could be no echoes, he felt like going back to the source of the Mondego, a little thread of water among some rocks almost at the top of the mountains, not that he found that thread, he remembered only moss, and there was no moss in the hospital, his father

—This is where the river Mondego begins

and he didn't believe him, a moist patch on the mountainside not even enough to make his cheeks damp, yellow petals, beetles, no bird making the tips of its wings tremble, how old would he have been, it wasn't a nurse who took his blood, it was Dona Irene, who played the harp in the evening and who called him Antoninho, the notary with a thousand pens in his jacket pocket, and possibly, among those pens, a couple of fingers too, would visit her after supper and, a few minutes later, they would hear the harp, the blood in the tube wasn't as red as he thought it would be but dark, if the bishop closed his eyelids he wouldn't say

—Not yet

he would say nothing, and Dona Irene pressed a piece of cotton wool to his arm and the notary's thousand pens glittered

—Antoninho

Dona Irene standing up

—I didn't hurt you, did I, my friend?

in a white gown and with a watch hanging upside down from a safety pin, if they operate on him tomorrow the gardener, not the doctor, will break his legs so that he'll fit in the hole with the mountains very clear in the distance, Dona Irene left the room shaking a tube and in it the sound of mattocks striking the earth, the telephone gesticulating in the corridor and a man's voice explaining

—Dr. Hélder has gone down to the surgical ward

the smell of his anxiety canceled out the smell of the hospital without canceling out the smell of the jam, Dona Irene

—The harp is all a question of touch

bracelets jingling, a question of touch, the six o'clock fast train made the glasses rattle and made the painting hanging

over the tea trolley shift slightly, at suppertime they would
bring Dona Lucrécia in from the porch

—A little bowl of chicken soup, Dona Lucrécia

and just as she began eating

—I'm tired

even if the following day, installed beneath the bottles in
the operating room, she were to wave her stick at him and
order him

—Come here, boy

and the porter who was pushing the gurney toward her
swollen legs and the crucifix on her black dress, if his grandmother put the straw hat on his head he wouldn't die, he
walked through the vineyard on the lookout for shells en-
crusted in the granite from the time when the sea covered
the world and the spirit of God, whatever that might be, hovered over the waters, next week, said the doctor, we can,
again the telephone ringing, the man's voice

—Dr. Hélder hasn't come back from the surgical ward yet

we can talk again when we have more facts, and while
we waited for the facts to arrive his grandmother was playing solitaire on the dining table, following the rows of cards
with her nose

—Can you by any chance spot the nine of clubs?

and what he could see was the queen of diamonds drying
herself beside the swimming pool, his heart hard to regulate
in secret, who would have thought it had so many tears in it,
hopefully they would fall inside rather than down his cheeks
as the anesthetist was asking him questions and he was saying to the anesthetist who wasn't drying himself on a towel

—Sorry

the electrocardiogram recording his tears on a strip of paper, what a drag, if he had an extra straw hat he could lend it to the anesthetist and show him the seashells from the time when the spirit of God hovered over the waters

—My mother cured everything with an aspirin

convinced that he had managed a smile that was even harder to regulate than his heart without anyone feeling astonished at the effort involved, yes, she cured everything with an aspirin, headaches, angina, fear of insects, insomnia, she didn't use a thermometer either, she would press her cheek to yours

—You're fine, son

and for a few seconds he could smell a sweet perfume and the savor of living flesh, the word *son* really meaning something, I'm your son and when I say "Mom" I'm saying something as true and real as the word *cup* or the word *ceiling,* though not the word *death,* if she pressed her cheek to mine now I might not believe her but it would help, the ox would breathe again despite the flies, don't break its legs, the mattock suspended in midair

—What's wrong, dear?

stray dogs hollow with hunger watching him or with their noses pressed to the pine needles sniffing for rabbits, they're probably trotting through the hospital looking for him, these people in the corridor aren't nurses, it's the dogs, their way of breathing, a pause dripping with drool, next week, said the doctor with the stain on his shoe that rather detracted from his air of competence, we'll talk when we have more facts, the mattock sliced through my legs, my grandmother's queen of spades appeared from beneath the king of diamonds and I bet he would have a stain on his shoe too if he existed below the waist, Dr. Hélder must have come back from the surgical ward now because the telephone fell silent, when he returned with his father to the Englishmen's hotel they were cleaning out the swimming pool and no one was there, he didn't pick up any balls that afternoon but squatted down in one corner feeling bored while the tops of the pine trees whispered secrets to one another, making the spots of sunlight shift about, one escaped from his trousers before he could catch it, he felt it on the back of his neck, made as if to trap it with his hand but lost it again, the certainty that he wouldn't sleep that night despite the pill in the little plastic cup, the pill slipped down into a fold in the sheet and instead of the pill there was the hospital stamp imprinted on the cloth, if his grandfather lent him his glasses he'd be able to find it, he remembered the sheets with the little bears on them when he was a kid, all the little bears so happy in their caps and scarves, they didn't have five fingers like us, but four, and four fingers were enough, thanks to those bears the illness had gone south, he felt like getting dressed and leaving in the rain

—The doctors were wrong

his grandmother used to sit listening to the trains in the cemetery, where the gravestones were so close together it was hard to squeeze between them, and she knew all the trains by the way they danced along the rails

—That's the eleven o'clock freight train, that's the four o'clock mail train

and yet despite the doctors being wrong a tightness, a nausea, an almost-pain that abates but remains, Dona Irene's harp a shudder taking on substance before being transformed into a shower of drops that fell on him and him still alive and cheerful beneath the drops, can you have cancer and be happy, no way, death did not come for him inside the music, because the drops were hiding him, just as they were hiding the chestnut trees and the house disguised by the ivy, his uncle blew his nose with great feeling and behind his handkerchief was another handkerchief as if he were a circus performer, dozens and dozens, hundreds of handkerchiefs and finally the national flag, his uncle in evening dress retreating behind a curtain amid much waving and bowing and with a dove perched on his shoulder, the tips of its wings trembling, the tightness transferred now to his spine, where his bones were crumbling, and the stain on the shoe pointing at they didn't quite know what on an X-ray

—I don't like the look of that vertebra

so I was wrong, they can break the ox's legs, don't shoot the dogs, Grandpa, shoot me, their drool, their hunger, not a single scream despite all the screams inside, every unmade gesture screaming, every movement of his head on the pillow screaming, every inch of skin screaming, so hard to conceal that fear, his grandfather always alone, the movements he made when he ate weren't like ours, he couldn't hear the chestnuts falling to the ground, every train was the same train and yet he did hear them just as he heard the perfume in the empty bottles and heard their weightless words calling

—Carlos

his godmother, his mother, ladies who existed so that we would stumble across them in the album while around them the world was advancing and retreating on some final beach, the time kept by the old clocks bearing no relation to ours because the hours were longer then, the dead continued to live in a parallel existence to this one in which furniture creaks strangely and the liquid in bottles oxidizes, my grandfather

—Who are you?

not understanding which age he belonged to, to that of his godmother and his mother or to ours, is that man in the hospital my grandson, the one clutching the tennis ball that the nurse gives him instead of a pill, while the wolves prowl around the school, there they are surrounding the bed, jaws gaping, and the bells from the goats in the mountains, another shower of drops that hide no one, less abundant, weaker, he hadn't imagined hospitals would be so bright, all plaster and metal, nor that suffering would be like this, his heart resisting regulation, resist, don't resist, resist, seven hours by the old clocks and how many hours inside him, crumpled up, twisted, he looks at the fingers clutching the sheet and what is a sheet worth, not a mica pebble or a tennis ball in the hand, or one of the chocolate mice they gave him as a child, with ears and whiskers drawn on the silver wrapping, if you eat a mouse the tightness will ease and you can sleep, perhaps you'll dream about the source of the Mondego and walk along by the rivers in a mist of light, I'm better now, the rabbits in the dismantled hutch are sure to gnaw away at the illness along with the weeds, and the stain on the shoe has gone, my grandfather's godmother

—Don't wake him up

not expecting that when he woke he would say

—Not yet

God who is in Australia or in China, not here, wondering what miraculous handle he should turn to restore sight to the blind and multiply the fishes, I'm afraid I might do it wrong and instead of multiplying the fishes cause the Red Sea to overflow and drown the Egyptians, the notes from the harp no longer shower down on the one who will spend the night staring at the window while his nausea grows, you're Senhor Antunes in bed eleven and Dona Irene stops playing the harp

—Antoninho

running her fingertips over a stringless void, the certainty that if she ran her fingers over his body he would start to sing, Dr. Hélder indifferent on the phone

—A waltz

and instead of Dr. Hélder the mattock breaking the ox's legs and Senhor Antunes's tendons, not Antoninho's, Antoninho is waiting on the grass by the pool, legs severed, Antoninho throwing stones at a scorpion pointing its poisonous stinger at him, worrying about the infinite number of dangers pursuing him, snakes, crows eager to peck out his heart, the whispering darkness warning him

—Don't you dare

while his bedroom, hidden from his parents, was squeezing and squeezing him, if he told them about the room, eyes lowered

—It won't happen again I promise

and a lit lamp, that's all it takes to stop them hurting him, the authority of lamps being far superior to that of the mayor with the gold tooth who dominated the domino games in the café, Senhor Antunes tried to rise to the surface of his sleep with the aim of making sure that the lamp was firmly screwed into the plaster ceiling and continued to protect him, the pillow a murmur of kapok

—The day before yesterday I saw a nest

and the storks were in fact disheveling the roof of the house, along with a small stone figure of a boy incapable of peeing into the lake full of litter and twigs, the ghost of a fish surfaced, then went back down again with the ghost of a protesting dragonfly in its mouth, the name Chalé Zulamira on a tiled plaque surrounded by sweet alyssum, the balcony on the second floor, no fancy wrought iron but a pot of hanging lilac, or possibly not lilac but tulips, or possibly not tulips, oh I give up, a pot of hanging plants, what does it matter if I'm going to die, the remnants of fabric that remain remember nothing, let alone the names of flowers, what suit will they dress me in, out of the three in the closet, the striped one, the wedding suit, the one with the darned sleeve, they'll take their time choosing the tie

—Which one, this one that he often used to wear and that I don't like or the blue one he never wore but that suited him better?

shoes polished and those enormous patent-leather clown's shoes, yes, he would rather like to wear those patent-leather shoes, with striped socks and a red nose, and to be handed a saxophone to play a paso doble while the family kept time clapping, Dona Irene

—Call that a musician

and an indignant wrinkle unnoticed by anyone on his painted cheeks, the doctor

—We'll operate on the clown with cancer tomorrow

and he doesn't ask

—What do clowns die from?

he says

—I know how clowns die

clowns, that is, once their bellies have been sliced open,

wearing enormous patent-leather shoes, despite having his saxophone taken away from him the paso doble grew louder, as you see, Grandpa, the chocolate mouse didn't help, I continue to look at the window and the tightness doesn't ease, it pretends it does but it doesn't, hopefully it will forget just as I forgot the names of the flowers on the balcony, not petunias, not dahlias, it doesn't matter, on the other hand, he didn't forget the lizard in the crack on the wall with its left legs forward and its head alert, this month or the next his name will appear on the obituary page with a cross above it, the station guard used to pile up bundles of newspapers with loads of crosses that were related to him and that no one noticed or if they did

—The deaf guy's nephew?

it could be the pharmacist or the lawyer with a toupee and no clients who used to sit on the esplanade doing crosswords and who lived off his wife, his toupee would sometimes come unstuck when he sweated and reveal a circle of glue, his wife resigned to it

—They didn't open my eyes in time

while the coarse-haired toupee slithered down to the back of his neck, if he rang the bell Dona Irene would appear dressed as a nurse with that watch hanging upside down, what happened to your harp, Dona Irene, oh, of course, a string was missing

—They didn't say I could give you another chocolate mouse, so you'll just have to wait

and so he looked at the window and the rain on the glass or at neither the window nor the glass, the gate over which he used to peer, perched on the sink in the laundry room, watching the maid getting undressed, he never mentioned the maid in confession or the blonde foreigner at the swimming pool and so maybe the illness was a punishment, the curate's housekeeper withdrawing her offer of grapes

—You have sinned

and him walking alongside the Mondego, now over this rock, now that one, and walking along beside the river, or more than one river, because it sometimes divided up only to join again, lost in the mist rising from the water and bushes and trees and tiny creatures, almost as skinny as he is now, slipping on the grass, sometimes he thought he'd fallen asleep but he was still awake along with his fears and his tears, certain he hadn't screamed despite all the screams inside, his uncle asking fondly

—What's wrong with the little fellow?

but how to find him in Lisbon, so far from the village, I haven't had any family for years, and his father is still playing tennis at the Englishmen's hotel and his mother is carefully parting his hair

—Stop fidgeting, silly

smelling different, old, looking in horror at her hands

—Are they mine?

a blouse that was too big for her now, eyes that didn't recognize him

—Who are you?

rings that belonged to his grandmother, so perhaps his mother would now be able to tell him about the trains, the midday one bringing the newspaper for his grandfather with his glasses and his fingers in his pocket, the mail train, the freight train, the fast train, his mother helpless and tiny in the deserted house, if he said

—Mom

a hesitant sideways glance, in the hospital the rain, the chestnut trees definitely black, the plate on the wall with an Our Lady painted on it coming off its hook, if his mother pressed her cheek to his, even when she was very old, even when blind, the word *son* would have real meaning, not the word *illness,* not the word *death,* as he walked beside the rivers, meeting no obstacles, accompanied by the paso doble played on a distant saxophone, and heading for the sea.

22 March 2007

The cart was all rattling wooden planks and creaking hinges on the bramble-lined path and he wasn't sitting up front with Virgílio, eager to be given the reins so that his grandmother

—My little prince

would understand who was in charge, he was lying in the back of the cart on top of a load of potatoes that were digging into his ribs, him pale in the shipwreck pallor of seven in the morning and not knowing whether the shipwreck was inside him or outside, Virgílio drove past hospital wards, screens, a wheelchair, not even noticing the hedges announcing the main door but noticing the rattling wooden planks and creaking hinges as they veered to the left and the mule moving more slowly over the linoleum with no ruts or stones, no bowls collecting resin from the pine trees, you cut into the bark with a small ax and the veins in the wood were long-drawn-out sadnesses, a woman wearing a green blouse, almost certainly an employee at the hotel where the Englishmen from the tungsten mines used to stay, pointed at Virgílio and said

—Put the stretcher there

and once again those rattling wooden planks, creaking

hinges, the stray potato that an old woman immediately snatched up and hid under her shawl, they eat them with the skin on, they don't even cook them, or they stick them in a hole covered with old clothes, more female hotel employees in green blouses lifted him onto his childhood bed but with no blanket and no pillow and he felt embarrassed to be lying naked beneath a starched sheet which far from covering his feet exposed them to the jeering lights, feet that seemed to him to belong to someone else, whose were they, the eucalyptuses spelling out the wind blowing around the hotel or was it people speaking, syllables that the treetops utter and that you then have to put together to form words, the word *surprise,* the word *terror,* the hotel employees came and went like a ballet of bees, Virgílio eyed them from the cart before leaving and then the brambles and the old woman who hid the potato under her shawl were lost, he thought his grandmother might help him by handing him a cookie

—My little prince

but the chestnut trees were so far away and the balcony facing the mountains was lost, all that was left was the pump on the well advancing and retreating without anyone moving it or just the sound lacerating the walnut trees, he saw the cook choosing a chicken to be killed and, in the study, the seascape while the pump was busy winching up surprise and terror, they're going to kill me, a needle in the arm that didn't feel like his and the syllables from the eucalyptuses coming faster now, announcing something but what, he felt sorry for his lonely feet at the mercy of the crows pecking at the trees in the orchard, one of the hotel employees placed a shell over his nose and mouth and all the surprise and terror became concentrated in his feet, under her shawl the old woman clutched the potato to her, greedily, fiercely, old women never used to talk, they limped along carrying the sacks of their bodies, he was amazed that the pump was so silent, the crows were cawing silently too, and the syllables uttered by the eucalyptuses and the hotel employees repeated that silence, Dona Irene's harp was inaudible, although the shower of drops was covering him again, separating him from the doctor, who was also wearing a green blouse, difficult to make out in the mist rising up from the Mondego, then the surprise and the terror left him, a primordial darkness filled his insides, reducing his life to incoherent colors and diffuse shapes vanishing down a drain he had not known existed inside him, and even though he wasn't thinking he thought he thought

—Who am I?

but what did *think* mean, what did *me thinking* mean or the me vanishing down the drain, he was sure the church bell was tolling and even though he knew it wasn't he continued to hear it dully tolling, the bell, the trains and his grandfather making an *O* with his mouth when he held out the spoonful of food to him, he didn't talk to anyone, he read the newspaper, walked in the vineyard or spent hours on the balcony not even looking at the mountains, he probably had an identical drain through which his life was escaping, transforming him into a ghost no one took any notice of, and yet there was a feeling still present in him that made him lean over the bed where his grandson could not see him while a knife was slitting open his belly to the rhythm of a circus paso doble with the family clapping in time

—They're operating on Antoninho

with someone else's feet and a tube down his throat that

one of the hotel employees was keeping an eye on, Antoninho feeling no surprise or terror, his cheeks not even wet with tears, and in losing who he was he lost the brambles flanking the path just as he lost the remnants of houses emerging from among the bushes, a fragment of a wall, a chimney, steps, Virgílio still not handing him the reins, for fear that the wheel might go down a ditch and buckle the axle, and his grandfather feeling in his pocket for his glasses so that he could examine him more closely, he remembered his grandfather's mother sitting sewing in her little wicker armchair with a blanket round her ankles, which they did not break when she died, the armchair continued to creak after she was in the cemetery and his uncle

—Whatever's wrong with that chair?

intrigued by how restless things were, what did they want, what did they want from us, the things in the kitchen growing deliberately old and warped

—They don't care about us, do they?

and certain jugs, certain jars, a certain trembling of the curtains trying to communicate who knows what and perhaps his grandfather understands as he observes him in the dining room of the Englishmen's hotel with the water pump of blood working, with retractors and forceps, the doctor with the stain on his shoe to the owner of the hotel showing him the spiky chestnut of the disease

—I don't know if I can detach it from the branch

among paintings of hunting scenes and pictures of horses, the workers falling ill in the tungsten mines and dozens of blonde foreigners leaving the swimming pool, his grandfather had died of the same cancer as him and, like him, with someone else's feet resting on the potatoes in the cart, Virgílio instead of

—Antoninho

ready to hand him the reins

—Here you are, sir

and his grandfather not even noticing the brambles or the remnants of the houses, thinking about a female cousin who called him

—Son

or about the wolves in winter and him perched on a rock watching them, because we're not in the hospital in Lisbon, we're near the spot where the Mondego begins, it isn't March, it isn't raining, listen to the music of the harp surrounded by equipment, X-rays and shiny instruments, no acrid smell of onion peelings in the kitchen, Doctor, and the lizard turned to stone, you don't think here, you keep going until the bell rings and the cemetery closes, the sacristan used to bolt the gate and the bent key in the rusty lock kept turning, what was his grandfather hearing in that void of silence, he was in the war in France when his daughter was born and when he returned from the war the silence had grown, the pendulum on the clock swayed silently, the wooden planks of the cart were silent, everything was simultaneously too remote and part of his body, and Dona Irene's harp was accompanying him in secret, no, not really accompanying him but bringing back the memory of the new young curate singing in Latin and the old ladies during mass hidden beneath their scarves, how are your potatoes doing, my grandson opening one eye on the dining table where they're operating on him, I don't feel upset for him, because if I met him in the square I wouldn't even know him, another skinny boy, another starving peasant, they dig up carrots from the vegetable plots, they steal firewood, he doesn't look anything like my daughter, he doesn't look anything like me either, judging by my wife's lips she's saying

—Antoninho

I gave him a chocolate mouse with ears and whiskers drawn on the silver wrapping and an inch of string as a tail because I didn't know what else to give him, go on, swallow the mouse to ease the pain, and him holding the mouse in his hand studying it, my daughter

—Aren't you going to eat it?

and the silly boy didn't eat it, convinced that the mouse was a living creature, when, apart from on the thick paper of photo albums, there are no living creatures left to make the tea and to worry about us, the mountains are alive too and never stop shifting about, swapping villages around, and as for us, I hardly dare say, Dona Irene's harp cutting through my deafness when I heard a pine cone fall and the ivy on the house telling its story in a nonexistent voice, and the owner of the hotel handing the chestnut to the employees, who wrapped it in a piece of cloth

—There are more chestnuts in here

and the surprise and the terror aren't in my grandson now, they're in me, the water pump of my heart beating so fast, dredging up only the remains of the shoe belonging to a drowned clown, I imagined that a saxophone would emerge after the shoe, the saxophone dissolved in the depths, I know about the sadness of things but not of people, and so I can't complain, besides what is sadness, I have no reason to feel sad, or there isn't the necessary space in my chest despite my being empty or, rather, not empty, because there's a candle in an old candlestick that the cousin who used to look after me placed on the bedside table, her hand on my forehead, promising me

—When you grow up you'll understand

I remember asking

—What is there to understand?

when I realized that only the candle was left in the room as well perhaps as me looking at it, how often I've asked myself if all this existed and if this place exists along with the vineyards, the trains and the silence interrupted by the miners or the old ladies and the goats grazing on rocks, the villages now populated either by creatures or by deserted ruins in which there was the persistent glow of a few small caves, I'm from here, I belong here, a cave or an old lady with my one potato stowed away in the lining of my jacket, a potato that I'll eat when no one's looking, the owner of the Englishmen's hotel pointing at my grandson's liver

—Another chestnut

emerging out of the darkness generated in the nucleus of light, why doesn't he just abandon it and forget it and put an end to surprise and terror, a teardrop on those painted cheeks becoming a scream, but all I hear are the harp and the murmurings from the photo album, footsteps that never approach, that only move farther off

—What did you die of, cousin?

realizing that as the candle is burning out, it flares up just before it burns out, then fades and does not rise again, I invented it, that candlestick, that candle, what night is this and what month, because the times all meld into one in the rain beating down on the acacia tree and beyond the acacia nothing but bushes and ditches

—Don't torment me, cousin

standing before my grandson, a lock of wet hair glued to his nose and his ears drained of color now that they've brought him back from the well, what endures in this place are the wells surrounded by walnut trees and in the wells a clown's shoe dissolved in the depths, what's left is the crucifix hating us because we were born and died beneath God's hatred, before the Englishmen of the tungsten mines the Germans of the tungsten mines, cartloads of tungsten being taken to the city, truckloads of tungsten, workers transporting baskets of tungsten, and the sound of boots and more boots passing the door accompanying a coffin that never ceases to pass, my coffin, my grandson's coffin, that of my mother before me, her wrists handcuffed by a rosary, the owner of the hotel was right, there are more chestnuts, and my grandson looking at the window and the rain, he couldn't drink, swallow, breathe, distancing himself from us and yet still believing in us

—I'm better, aren't I?

a contented idiot, a hopeful fool, with the pain still flourishing, not bothering him, because he's become used to it, even if it gets worse he doesn't notice, even if he becomes a grown-up again he doesn't feel it, everywhere the smell of tungsten, not the illness, and the sound of boots and more boots beneath a bell that stopped ringing centuries ago, the same one that accompanies me on the balcony, penetrates the newspaper I'm not reading and pursues me and catches me, how can I hear it if the footsteps inhabit me and in the midst of them I too am walking, someone whispers

—It's over

and the mountains devouring the house and Virgílio's cart with its broken left wheel, the curate's housekeeper absent from the porch although one part of her remains, holding out a bunch of grapes to the flower beds, the village a place that the bushes will cover along with brambles and bits of granite, not to mention the mountain winter that makes the villages disappear, there's the place where we lived, a fragment of wall, a chimney, steps that the harp will continue to adorn, my cousin's hand on my head

—When you grow up you'll understand

no train at the station, where piles of newspapers are waiting, not that I ever read them, and in the midst of the granite and the pine trees the Englishmen's hotel intact, in the dining room my grandson beneath the lamps and the owner of the hotel wearing a green mask, why is everything green in August, insects, frogs and the flock of partridges on the gorse-covered slopes, the grandson whom my wife calls

—Antoninho

and then the cook slitting a duck's throat and throwing the feathers into the same bucket where the owner of the hotel was throwing the gauze compresses, the ox's legs broken with the mattock and, trotting through the orchard, the mule whose eyes had been gouged out with a knife by a laborer my father had dismissed, at the hospital window in Lisbon the rain and the presence of death in every squeak and whistle from the goods lift, the pain immaculate until we plunge into it, and as we plunge in a shock, we barely notice and then we're floating free in the density of peace, the oxygen bottle turned off, the serum flowing into our motionless arm, my stone deafness while the fingers of Dona Irene freeze over the harp strings and the owner of the pharmacy stands outside his store smoking, Virgílio died before me, in February, separated from the mountains by the fringe of clouds, the old ladies stole his saucepans, his clothes, and he, like me, didn't hear a thing, alone in the still-sighing gloom, I remember a harness hanging from a nail and in a tiny corner of me the cousin with the candle saying

—When you grow up you'll understand

boots and more boots outside the main door, the same ones pounding away today in my deafness confining me forever to the sofa, conversations I don't hear, gestures I don't notice just as I preferred not to notice my grandson's face in the Englishmen's hotel, I knew that his face was my face and those feet were mine, I should put a candle on his bedside table so that the trains begin to run again down below and a piece of mica glitters in the sun, reassuring him

—When you grow up you'll understand

confiding

—When you grow up you'll understand

and the chestnut trees spending all night discussing how the earth despises us and ends up dismissing us, I could feel my wife beside me in bed and I moved away from her because I could sense she was listening to the things insistently whispering

—You don't belong here anymore

to these stones, this scrub, these trees devouring us with cruel haste just as the bushes and the granite are devouring us, we are shells empty of any echo, snail shells that turn to dust if we touch them, the damp from the moss around the Mondego that is constantly being born in a crack in the rocks, I died of the same illness as him but not in Lisbon, in the village, hearing the footsteps setting the world trembling and waiting on my pillow for the old ladies to come in, the bell not tolling but sounding the fire alarm, and workers with unfinished faces, which is what happens to the poor left incomplete by hunger, racing along tunnels carrying buckets, the owner of the Englishmen's hotel pointing at my grandson

—He might have a few more months

and what are a few months worth

—When you grow up you'll understand

a lie, a falsehood, I don't understand anything at all with those never-changing mountains I can see from the balcony and the jackdaws leaving the eucalyptuses presaging dusk, my mother would light all the lamps and the furniture would stand out in unexpected relief, they killed the blind mule and the creature slid to the ground revealing its gums and its large soft teeth, making me think of a train, not a freight train, the postmen delivering letters I will never see, possibly from my sister-in-law in the sanatorium

—He's feverish, Carlos

wrapped in a blanket, the owner of her hotel would drop by at the end of the day to listen to her lungs

—Very good, very good

and the lightness of the snow, I do remember that, making the pine trees denser, one of the employees said to someone behind me, the man in charge of luggage, the receptionist, the porter

—Call the cart to take him to the recovery room

and I noticed that the Mondego was gathering strength with every downward hump and bump because it was being joined by the water from other rocks, not a single river but four or five that came and went, propelling my grandson's life and mine, we no longer are, we were

—He might have a few months left

until September, when I was leaning on the balcony rail and the shade cast by the ivy suddenly revealed me, one of my children saying

—Dad

and I knew that

—Dad

even if I couldn't hear, I could hear the chestnut trees murmuring, murmuring, the front door opening, then immediately closing again, the cart all rattling wooden planks and creaking hinges on the bramble-lined path and now and then the remnants of a house, my grandson sitting not up front with Virgílio, hoping he would give him the reins, but in the back of the cart on top of the potatoes digging into his ribs in the shipwreck pallor of seven o'clock in the morning, uncertain as to whether the shipwreck was inside him or outside, on the gray expanse of the final beach, and what do I know of beaches, where a single seagull was flying indifferently along, Virgílio drove past hospital wards, screens, a wheelchair, my grandson didn't notice the wheelchair, he noticed the rattling wooden planks and the creaking hinges veering to the left and the mule moving more slowly over the linoleum with no ruts or stones, no bowls collecting resin from the pine trees, you cut into the bark with a small ax and the veins in the wood were long-drawn-out sadnesses, my grandson with someone else's feet and no need of them, people, quite who I don't know, must live here, the tungsten mine will be exhausted one day and there'll be no Englishman staying in the hotel, they'll change the sheets on the hospital bed, they'll take away the oxygen, the IV drip, the machine that records on a strip of paper the movements of the water pump and the drops from the harp, who will break his legs with a mattock so that he fits in the hole and what worms will come looking for him under the earth, I came up from the vineyard to the porch and somewhere inside me, some clear insignificant point, my cousin with the candlestick and the candle still repeating

—When you grow up you'll understand

however insistently my children

—Dad

shook my arm I found myself by the waters of the Mondego, which were ceaselessly dividing and joining up again, I realized that I had died many years ago or rather not just me but everything that was and no longer exists, adrift on the water floating far away from all of you.

23 March 2007

Shapes, shapes. Shapes that came and went and came again, overlapping then moving off, turning slowly or rising up only to subside, seeming to become more defined but instead dissolving, the illusion of voices and nonvoices, presences and nonpresences, that of his mother, for example, who even while she was asleep could hear the cat's tail twitching

—Can you hear the cat's tail twitching?

and there the cat was among the delicate porcelain, the teacups vibrating, the cat's tail twitching loudly then stopping, and his mother

—I can't hear anything now

he tried to give a name to the shapes but couldn't find any, he both was and wasn't awake just as happens the moment when we seem to have grasped the meaning of the universe and the meaning vanishes, the cat whose eyes were reborn after every yawn, yes, shapes, he couldn't feel anything, he wasn't thinking about anything, he was simply there, shapes of words too, shapes of sounds, a bulb turning on and turning off and more shapes, bulbs, tastes, smells, he had no body, he was just a shape among the other shapes, a cube, a pyramid, a sphere among cubes, pyramids and spheres, a pale window that gradually took on substance and his mother raising a part of him up out of the puddle in which he lay

—Doesn't even the cat's tail wake you up?

a kind of pincer pinching his arm, a face right in front of his, not his mother's face

—He's beginning to come round

and if it wasn't his mother's face whose was that face vanishing like the meaning of the universe that always eluded him, mysteries too simple for him to find, what he found now without touching it was his leg, there it was, at least he had one leg among the shapes that came and went and came again and he felt sorry to lose them, not his leg, though, that was solid, fixed, too far away for him to be able to move it, if it wasn't just a shape he would cheer up, drops not on his skin but suspended in the air around him, making the shapes larger, and what he had assumed was a window turned out to be a wall or rather a surface swimming with shadows like the dappled shade on the cart as it moved along, the trees full of leaves also trying to decipher the meaning of the universe, he tried to shut that meaning up inside him and sneak off toward the leg or the mouth that was beginning to exist, or rather an area that he called mouth because he could feel what seemed to him to be teeth, the beginning of a tongue and a tube touching the teeth and the beginning of a tongue, a protuberance he thought was a shoulder and the shapes continuing to spin, now green now blue now white now completely colorless and even the colorless color was a color, he asked

—What do you call a colorless color?

aware that the question, like his tears, was meaningless, he needed to teach what he called a mouth to be a mouth with a tongue and real teeth, saliva, gums, to construct a proper nose or a nose shape, shapes, shapes that came and went and came again, overlapping and moving off, turning slowly, seeming to become more defined but instead dissolving, the illusion of voices and nonvoices, presences and nonpresences, that of his mother, for example, who even while she was asleep

—Can you hear the cat's tail twitching?

and him separated from the shapes by a transparent curtain about to disappear, to construct a nose that could connect to his mouth and perhaps to his ears, his head, his whole body, but he lacked fingers, beyond his leg and his shoulder his belly growing, among the dappled shade of the trees something like a cloud, a fragment of a bird not knowing which part of it was missing as it left its branch, shapes and in the middle of those shapes his mother

—Doesn't even the cat's tail wake you up?

not the one today trying to make out who he was

—If you speak I'll know who you are

his mother from long ago, capable of dealing with frying pans, earrings and scissors that refused to obey him, they would fall to the ground before he even touched them convinced that he had touched them, really touched them

—You frightened them off

the face bending over him

—He's beginning to come round

however, it wasn't the face he could see but a machine monotonously drawing lines, not even a shape, just lines that would reach the edge of the screen then start again, over and over, he felt like repeating his mother's words

—If you speak I'll know who you are

and then a sigh, a whisper, a handful of cartilages, organs that were waking up, each with their respective souls and timbres, a muscle contracting and it was his whole arm, although he wasn't clear that it was an arm, Virgílio turning to him in the cart

—We've arrived

not words, shapes of words and the trees and the sky, the potatoes digging into his back, the cook picking up walnuts and collecting them in her skirt, but what was missing was his grandfather with his newspaper and the perfume from the eucalyptuses, because it seemed to him that it was a perfume, not a smell, smell was for potatoes and perfume for the eucalyptuses, and so he wasn't in the house where they spent the summer, he wasn't in August, he was in Lisbon, where the Mondego doesn't begin and there are no rocks and no moss, chestnuts begin there, and he couldn't feel their spines even though he knew they were still waiting in ambush in his insides like a vixen tense and ready to pounce and he was convinced that with one leap, teeth, claws

—Good God, I'm a rabbit

the doctor with the stain on his shoe or rather the doctor who didn't know he had a stain on his shoe because he existed only from the waist up

—Don't speak

as if speaking might disrupt some complicated harmony and as if the shapes might multiply around him and strangle him, cubes, pyramids, spheres, the second leg along with the first and the bird perched on a whole branch now, nurses, beds, the whiteness of a limitless morning in which time was not even suspended, there was no time, him still incapable of hearing the cat's tail

—Can you hear the cat's tail?

as blind as his mother looking for herself among the blurred trees or what she thought were blurred trees

—What distinguishes you from me, Mom?

or slowly undulating shoals of fish

—What am I doing here?

not realizing what had happened to him nor where he had returned from, entering and leaving his body in a vapor of truncated memories, remembering the curate's house-keeper and the elms in the square, why did the doctor say

—Don't speak

when it was only by speaking, even if he couldn't form sentences, that he could be sure he existed, if I keep silent I don't exist, perhaps the rain would throw a final shroud over his mutilated belly, people in the ward ignoring him and him wanting to beg them please think of me, help me, but they weren't interested and they didn't help him, or only his grandfather did, he had died forty years ago, though, but how could he have died forty years ago if he was there, his grandfather for whom eucalyptuses, nostalgia and fam-ily were mere shapes as well, shapes that came and went and came again, overlapping and then moving off, turning slowly or rising up only to subside, seeming to become more defined but instead dissolving, he tried to give them a name but couldn't find one, the surprise and terror returned while his mother

—I can't hear the cat, dear

because Dona Irene's harp or the lindens were interrupting him, he remembered the vet's wife sitting on a bench smiling at a book, so that when they took his hand he thought it was her, her hair lit up by the sun, if the vet's wife were to touch him he would fall to pieces and his father testing the strings on his tennis racket

—Why would you fall to pieces?

not that he really cared, he would die the way pigs do, unaided, a knife in the jugular and bye-bye, they would pour gasoline over him and strike a match to scorch his skin, asking

—Do you feel all right?

and even though he could respond now that his voice was working again he remained silent, searching with what was left of his mind for the person who had asked the question, the trellis, the chicken run, the cat's tail he could hear in the dark, not even animals died alone, he remembered his mother stroking the cat until its breathing stopped, its tail rose up and his mother did not

—Can you hear the cat's tail twitching?

but silently sniffing the air, a vein in the neck beating faster than a thrush's heart, shapes that stopped coming and going, overlapping, moving off, the word *cancer* and along with that word disconnected images, him in the dentist's chair thinking about the sea and the way the sand glittered before the seagulls arrived

—Do you feel all right?

and I really do feel all right, it doesn't hurt in the least, I can see the sea that Virgílio never saw just as he never saw the Mondego because the mountains with their vast peaks frightened him, he simply unharnessed the mule and sat down among the empty sacks to drink a bottle of wine, it wasn't only the mountains that frightened him, it was the men who lived there and who, in turn, never came down to the village, or very occasionally a child or a billy goat that had given up trying to walk along a fence, he said

—Yes, I'm all right

so that they would leave him to ponder and he did feel all right, he thought perhaps I'm better although without believing that he was, and the indignity of the illness offended him, if the men from the mountains fell ill with a fever they would bury themselves alive, that is, they would dig a hole, lie down in it and stare up at the people heaping them with clods of earth, perhaps Virgílio was right, there were only dead people up there and the lights in the darkness were all that remained of the deserted villages, since there were no windows he didn't know if it was still raining outside, it was still March but what year was it given that time was a continuum full of other people's memories, memories belonging to the creatures in the other beds, just as his memories were perhaps filling theirs, relatives he didn't know, someone or other handing him a little basket of small pears

—Here you are, Artur

then realizing his mistake and taking back the basket

—Sorry

then apologizing and offering him a pear

—Please, I insist

rubbing it on his sleeve to improve the color

—My brother-in-law won't mind, go on, take one

his mother saying to his uncle

—Can you really not hear it?

explaining that she meant the cat and his uncle asking

—Does it really make a noise with its tail?

the four o'clock mail delivery passed with no letters for him, give me back the pine trees, the mountains, the childhood that I brought to the hospital and that belongs to me, the vet's wife smiling at her book, no one was playing the piano in the attic and yet from somewhere came a secret polka, him calling to his mother

—Listen, Mom, a polka

his mother cupping one hand to her ear

—What polka?

he opened the piano lid and the strings were quite still

—Where can that sound be coming from, then?

and it came from the little boy who had played the wrong notes, the teacher making him start all over again

—Will you never learn?

he occasionally dropped asleep and once again the shapes overlapping then moving off, turning slowly or rising up only to subside, seeming to become more defined, and he

—Grandpa

amazed that his own mouth could speak

—Grandpa

when his grandfather could do nothing, he looks at the newspaperless balcony, he looks at the deserted vineyard, his glasses lying useless on the dresser and when he puts them on, the furniture's all crooked

—Is that how you saw the house, Grandpa?

shapes and shapes, the illusion of voices and nonvoices, presences and nonpresences, he tried to give a name to the shapes and couldn't find one, the creature in the next bed stopped moaning because the mountain men had strangled

him and there was nothing but gorse, the vet's wife closed
her book and smiled and he remembered how his mother
whenever she mentioned her would say

—That woman

would shake her head, tell me what happened to the vet's
wife, her husband would sit on the balcony with Grandpa
on a Sunday while the mist on the mountains blurred the
villages, his wife not under the lindens smiling at the sun-
flowers in the garden, he didn't know why that smile brought
back his illness without Dona Irene's harp there to protect
him, every string a painfully twanging nerve, a hotel employee adjusted the drip in his arm and her nostrils seen
from the pillow were gigantic, another employee was plucking chickens in the back room and the feathers were spiral-
ing around him so that the feathers were in the hospital too
only they never touched the ground, in October he would
come back from church pursued by leaves and each leaf was
a cancer, each feather a cancer, each drop of serum a cancer, death circling him beneath a catastrophic sky, the sound
of boots and more boots out in the street, if a bell rang they
would bring a screen and behind the screen there would be
lots of hustle and bustle and murmurings, the anxious lights
blinking out signals, he asked them

—What's up?

because if he knew that he wouldn't die, and more cubes,
more pyramids, more spheres would block his life, he
thought he had shooed the shapes away with the arm with
the IV drip but instead of scattering they grew in number,
the blonde foreigner walked back and forth in his head for
a moment like a secret candle and the tops of the maples
made her more real, promising him

—You're alive

of course he was alive, neither the boots nor the tolling bell nor the open coffin were meant for him, his mother whispering in his ear

—Can you hear the cat's tail?

one finger on her lips telling him to keep quiet because the cat was a matter that concerned only them, shapes, shapes coming and going and coming again, overlapping and moving off, spinning slowly or rising up and quickly subsiding, how absurd all this is, call Virgílio to take him back home in the cart rattling down the bramble-lined path, now and then a patch of sunlight on the walls, and the memory of the jar of candy filled him with emotion, he was back in the village, not in Lisbon, the proof being the perfume of eucalyptuses, horseflies, rocks, the doctor saying to the employee plucking the chicken

—Tomorrow or the day after we'll have him moved to the ward

and the wolves crouched on the grass opposite him in the hospital corridor, his mother in nostalgic mood

—How you've grown

and the cat's tail echoing loudly through the house, voices that weren't voices, presences that weren't presences, a kind of dream that was simultaneously incoherent and precise, the doctor removed the dressing to examine the wound

—Let's wait and see what the result of the specimen is

and how odd to call his illness a specimen, to examine it under a microscope, to write about it, him reduced to a name and a number, not even a shape, at the top of the page the name they've forgotten, which means he doesn't exist, what exists is the description of what they called the specimen and that's all they were concerned about, not him, him sitting on the balcony where his grandfather used to sit with the newspaper waiting for the midday train, or strolling in the vineyard beneath the March clouds, and when he thought of the clouds he would have bet anything that it hadn't stopped raining since yesterday, his last memory would be the drops of rain on the window, not people, not the village, drops racing down toward the windowsill, followed by more drops and more drops and then new drops following those other drops in a perpetual winter, and another specimen watching the rain instead of him with the same feeling of surprise and terror, his mother with the cat on her lap

—Can you hear his tail twitching?

when what he could hear was the six o'clock fast train arriving from the city and on it the major's widow with whom his father would hold whispered conversations, Dona Lucrécia on the porch

—Come here, boy

her plump hand beckoning, don't respond, run, the major's widow saying to his father at the far end of the garden

—Darling

and the blinds coming down, his father standing among the lemon trees that were threatening to tell everyone

—Oh yes, we'll tell everyone, you can be sure of that

his grandmother drying his mother's tears with her handkerchief

—Don't fret, that's what men are like

if only he were a man in the eyes of that blonde foreigner in the Englishmen's hotel instead of a child clutching a tennis ball, his father coming into the house, asking the cook for a bowl of hot water and him vanishing in among the steam, he could just make out a sponge and a bent back and his father from beneath the towel

—What are you doing here?

but he wasn't doing anything, he was simply amazed, he tried to use the razor but he had no beard, tried to make a part but his hair was all over the place, he went into the garden belonging to the widow and the lemon trees

—Stupid boy

crochet curtains and the clock's pendulum bowing deeply, one of his father's shoes on one side, the other lost, and his father grappling with the buckle on his belt

—The damned thing's stuck

not barefoot, in socks with a little hole in one of them, the widow deeply moved by the sight

—Shall I sew it up for you, sweetheart

kneeling down in a flowery dressing gown with, underneath, lots of ribbons and bows, his grandmother praising her despite her adultery

—She studied at a college in Porto

the widow slowly removing his father's socks, her left hand the fork and her right hand the knife, as delicately as if she were extracting a fish bone

—Mary Magdalene did the same for our Lord

more perfectly than his grandmother cutting the fish in half and putting the skin and the head on a smaller plate because the sight of them disgusted him

—You can eat now

while his grandfather pursued the bones with his tongue, his whole being probing about between gums and cheek, finding the bone, losing it, finding it again and then cautiously funneling it through to his lips, picking it up with two fingers, rubbing them together to get rid of it, drying them on his napkin and starting the search all over again

—I've never seen so many damn bones

the only words I heard him say in the twelve years I lived with him, as soon as he put down his cutlery and began his maneuvers the whole family put down their cutlery too, tense and waiting, my grandmother would grab me by the elbow in a foretaste of funerals to come, then let out a jubilant sigh

—He did it

and the mountains, equally relieved, grew larger, my father's feet in complex, strange positions

—Darling

and the major looking benignly down from his photo, not like my grandmother's ancestors, who were all trembling with rage, the dedications on the back written in such sharp calligraphy that if you touched them they bit you, perhaps what my grandfather kept removing from his mouth were inscriptions, not fish bones, in the widow's bedroom my father was another pendulum bowing low

—Jeez

accompanied by a dozen or more

—Darling

small languid fluttering wings, him remembering his grandmother drying his mother's tears with her handkerchief

—Don't fret, that's what men are like

or in the presence of that blonde foreigner at the Englishmen's hotel and his disappointed reflection in the swimming pool

—I'll never be a man

his feet would never adopt strange positions, he would never use a steam bath, he could hear the cat's tail twitching, he liked candy, he was afraid of centipedes, Dona Lucrécia

—Come here, young man

no, that's a lie

—Come here, boy

him sitting next to his mother in the church pew and his father so perfectly at ease with God that he didn't even bow his head during the Elevation of the Host but regarded the Host on an equal footing, how could the blonde foreigner ever call him

—Darling

when he was so small, so feeble, incapable of driving the cart down the bramble-lined path and therefore sitting not next to Virgílio but in the back with the potatoes, watching the pine trees go by and what was left among the weeds of the old chapel, if the hotel cook were to start plucking him now he would simply accept it, the blonde foreigner put away her various sun creams and left slowly in the hope that he would follow her, alas, he couldn't

—I'm only eight years old, Senhora

and the blonde foreigner

—Eight years old?

then flounced off angrily down the boxwood-lined path.

24 March 2007

Just as he had as a child, he had felt sure that he would never die or turn into a portrait framed by a sigh, he thought the trains that ran past the far side of the vineyard, the freight train and the fast one, and the four o'clock mail train, would sometimes carry only the driver and the stoker, and today in the hospital, with a chestnut lodged in his body, he realized that the trains that no longer stopped at the station where they used to deposit his grandfather's newspaper and the occasional locked and secret trunk were all empty, lines of deserted cars coming from who knows where and heading to who knows what, windows ablaze in the night and vacant by day, and he realized then that the story his grandfather used to tell him in order to make him finish his soup, about a little girl who would ask at every stop

—Did Antoninho eat his lunch?

telling the grown-ups

—If he didn't I might cry, you know

was a lie, no one was crying over him, the only truth was the chestnut growing inside him and him calculating the areas it was occupying one by one, if the little girl existed she would be clutching a soft toy and sobbing her heart out and he, feeling sorry for her and for himself, would be running through the cars calling to her, he wasn't looking at the hospital windows now, so as to forget about the rain, and not bothering the nurses either, so as to forget they were there, leaving behind him the mountains the Mondego the alder trees and the birds, his father

—You see, Antoninho, it's already a river

as they peered into the water in which twigs twisted and turned, a father different from the one he knew saying to him

—You know

then regretting having spoken, speak, Dad, before a ragged piece of night interposes itself between us, the chestnut in his ears preventing him from hearing just as he cannot hear the little girl calling to him from the past, everything in him alive apart from him, the hotel employees and the trains keeping time with his alarmingly fast heartbeat, the father who three years before had been transformed into a profile, they phoned from the Clinic and his nose was motionless, no tennis ball jumped over the fence and so there was no need to go looking for it in the bushes, he thought

—You know

but the father-turned-portrait with no sigh to frame him, the bright brambles in the Clinic garden, in the closet, in the bed, on his lips a last

—You know

perhaps unspoken, tell me your secret, help me, I stumble through the cars not seeking but escaping from the thing I carry within me, the brambles were making the blanket expand and contract as if my father were shifting about beneath it and the Clinic was a Lisbon train heading off into the mountains, what happened to the certainty that I won't die, the curate

—What do you mean you won't die?

lifting up the hem of his cassock to avoid the puddles, revealing bony shins, the trains set off empty and the room set off with them swaying through the trees, in the villages a level crossing and a peasant woman carrying firewood on her head standing watching, he could do with a chocolate mouse to help him cope with the fear, don't just stand there holding the mouse, eat it, he remembers his grandmother stroking his neck

—What will become of you?

and the ring with the little silver bow, how old were you, sixty, seventy, the doctor deciphering bits of paper

—Let's consider our options

and for a few seconds a foolish optimism, ready to color a word, a smile, his grandfather rejecting the newspaper and his mother disappointed

—Won't you at least have a little soup?

bring him a chocolate mouse and he might accept it, gazing delightedly at its whiskers and ears, open your mouth when you hold out the spoon so that he'll open his as well, no neck now, no strings, no glittering claws, the ivy growing on the balcony didn't seem particularly keen when his uncle taught him to ride a bike between the chestnut tree and the gates, trotting along beside him holding on to the saddle

—Keep pedaling

his uncle left behind him exhausted while he all alone was heading straight for the garage unable to brake, the garage suddenly enormous and his uncle so very far away

—Stop

he passed one flower bed, then another, the doctor

—Let's consider our options

and he felt contented even though the incision was beginning to bother him, this isn't pain yet, it's on the way to
becoming pain, and in a few hours it would become pain,
impossible to apply the brakes despite his uncle's cries, a
tree root knocked the front tire off course and it wasn't the
main gate now but a granite pillar with an urn on top, his
grandfather distracted by the chocolate mouse couldn't see
him from the living room, his grandfather wearing slippers
he didn't even know existed, for he had always been properly shod until then, how white this room is and how troubling the whiteness that the blackness of the chestnut was
filling up with spines, everything black and white, what happened to the other colors, where's the suit I wore to the hospital and my wristwatch and my wallet, I'm afraid of the
whiteness, grab the saddle and stop that pillar growing bigger and bigger as I approach, my grandfather is wearing not
a linen jacket or serge trousers but a pajama jacket with the
buttons all buttoned up the wrong way and him feeling sorry
for his grandfather

—Grandpa

the suspicion of footsteps in the hospital, the curate, a
bell, beyond the raindrops on the window the drops of serum that were slow to fall, the approaching pain advancing
and receding, abandoning him as it left behind other pains
he thought he'd forgotten, the piece of wire they stuck in his
finger and the disinfectant, a cruel screw going down to the
bone, the girl who didn't reply to his letters and how for a
month or two, it makes him smile now, he felt tempted to
kill himself, despite the speed the bike was going at, how to

explain this, he struck the granite pillar very slowly, hitting head and elbows on the stone and all this in silence, his uncle by his side

—Don't move

and the bike frame pressing down on his hip, he thought he heard his mother

—Who are you?

when he visited her on Tuesdays he didn't know if he was visiting her or his own past even though he found it hard to recognize himself in a place where there was no trace of what he had been, only images of images and rooms more deserted than the trains, the doctor

—Let's consider our options

let's consider our options, how stupid, it might be a better idea to turn into a portrait framed by a sigh, his grandfather helped him up

—No broken bones

and again the perfume of the eucalyptuses, Dona Lucrécia on the porch and the curate pruning the bougainvilleas, his mother couldn't remember the chestnut trees or the well, if you talked to her about the village while she was stroking the cat she would immediately stop

—Yes, it's true

what's true, Mom, there are no pots and pans no gold jewelry at the fair now, the bicycle bell a sad little tinkle, a desire for someone to stroke the arm with the IV drip, to hold his hand, the trains at the far end of the vineyard and which he thought were full of people but were in fact empty, the nurse taking his temperature

—In a week's time you'll be absolutely fine

like the deserted cars rusting away under the trees growing ever taller on a branch line of stations whose names he doesn't recall and where the vixens and the genets dig their nests, his mother

—The well

and thinking about the well helped him fall asleep for a few minutes, distancing himself from the chestnut, you're right, nurse, in a week's time I'll be absolutely fine or else riding my bike around the trunk of the tree, his uncle

—Do a figure eight

the granite pillar inoffensive, complicit, his uncle still telling him

—Do a figure eight, Antoninho

and there he was doing figure eight after figure eight next to the hotel swimming pool with the blonde foreigner saying approvingly

—Darling

not in Portuguese, of course, but in her own language, and even though he couldn't understand, he was sure she was saying

—Darling

with one shoe on one side, the other lost, clothes on the floor, he didn't care which bush the tennis ball was under

—I'm a man now

even though his father

—Are you going to bring me that ball today?

what did he care about the ball, go and fetch it yourself, I'm busy, I can't, women's skin so soft and them eagerly saying yes, take off my swimsuit, undress me, show the swimming pool who's in charge, when they open their eyes afterward they're not with us, they're returning from some unknown place, they take a while to recognize us and when they do

—Darling

submissive, grateful, indolent, all fluttering eyelids and garbled words, the nurse

—Excellent

and him almost saying

—Garbled words

but stopping in time

—Sorry I fell asleep

aware that the rain had stopped, raindrops forming part of the window with no new drops falling, the urine in the catheter felt as if it didn't belong to him, it merely passed through him, much as memories and ideas were passing through him, the remote past, the alien present, the non-existent future, cars and cars without wheels or doors traveling along a branch line, if they asked him his name he would hesitate, if he had a name the catheter would carry it off into the drainage bag and he would again be left without a name, the bicycle in the bag, his grandmother in the bag, his mother in the bag

—Who are you?

touching his face

—I don't know you

strange though it may seem, and it did seem strange, I was born out of you, I lived with you, I died, everything is leaving me, draining me dry, abandoning me, and meanwhile Dona Lucrécia

—Come here, boy

it's impossible for Dona Lucrécia to disappear, she'll last forever, there was an ash tree in her garden that used to frighten the sparrows, if a bird approached, the tree would swallow it up just as the illness was swallowing him, they had put a diaper on him and he didn't find that odd, they washed him with a washcloth and his private parts wobbled uselessly about, the blonde foreigner from the swimming pool

—Is that thing you?

the thing they wrapped up again and him not even

—Yes, that's me

resigned, saying to the doctor

—Do whatever you like

and that's fine, the moist air from the source of the Mondego on his forehead, rocks, gorse, an alder tree full of catkins

—Are you going to bring me that ball today?

he would grope around among the box hedges, his father pointing with his racket

—More to the left

and even though he was sure it wasn't, he rummaged around to the left, getting scratched in the process, the hotel owner checking the lines on the screen

—Are you feeling better, my friend?

no, the hotel owner

—Did you find the ball?

no, the hotel owner saying to the nurse

—Did you tell him that in a week's time he'll be absolutely fine?

performing figure eights on his bike and when he entered the tungsten mine nothing but echoes, too many peasants in their holes in the village, so many peasants in the hospital with him, so many old ladies in black watching him, between the mountains and the sky the bright line that precedes morning and one or two red kites unable to find the path, the darkness begins in the valleys, fig trees shrinking, not a breath of wind, the teacher telling them to open their exercise books, announcing

—Dictation

and him crouched over the clean page

—Title "The balloon"

the slide in the playground, let's hope there still is a slide there, something else that lasts and not just the shadow of the mountains, he didn't look out the hospital window, because of the rain, and the possibility that the orchard might feel glad just to see him made him feel awkward, the pears, the apples, the cherry tree still in blossom, he thought that in a matter of weeks there would be cherries and the blossom would be gone, a sum not quite erased from the blackboard, maps with the dots of cities and the veins of rivers, every province a different color, the sea to the left, a space to the right with the word *Spain* written not horizontally but vertically and a squashed insect on the last letter, I don't believe there are no trains leaving and no grapes rotting on the vines, I don't believe I will die, I recognize the diapers, the catheter, the pain, the chestnut, but it doesn't make sense, me dying, and because it doesn't make sense I'm going to stay, even if

—He's died

I'm going to stay even if I stop breathing, the drip stops dripping and the line on the screen goes flat, I'm going to stay, my mother will find me

—Antoninho

and so I did stay, after the sale of the house here I am, after another patient has taken my place here I am, relegated to a corner but still here, with no one noticing me but here, the teacher

—New line Brought to life by a child's cheeks

and the proof is that there I was, in the depths of despair, brought to life by a child's cheeks, chekes, chiques, cheex, a child's cheaks brought me to life, no, a child's chekes brought me to life, a child's cheex brought me to life, my chiques never brought life to a single balloon, I was too afraid it might burst, too afraid of loud bangs, too afraid of balloons, you just gave them a poke with your finger and off they floated, string waving, always changing direction, falling so very delicately, wobbling, stopping, brought to life by a child's cheeks pursuing him from when he was just seven years old, viscous, tenacious, don't give me a chocolate mouse now, I might fall asleep before the dictation, I don't want my parents to receive a letter from the school and then punish me, I want to go zooming down the slide into the sandbox and then jump to my feet, if the doctor were to ask me

—How are you feeling, my friend?

I would say

—Cheak

no, I would say

—Brought to life by a child's cheeks

proud because I hadn't made a single mistake in my dictation, how can an illness compare with being brought to life by a child's cheeks, what are metastases compared with a sphere that swims slowly, weightlessly along, with Victoria's For Everything the Modern Woman Needs printed on it, by the second day the sphere was beginning to shrivel, by the third it needed a child's cheeks to bring it to life again, my mother snipped off the string and the balloon became a mere rag, Victoria's For Everything the Modern Woman Needs shrunk to almost nothing, she blew hard, stopped halfway, keeping the lip of the balloon closed shut with her two fingers

—It's hard work

she started blowing again until Victoria's For Everything the Modern Woman Needs was once again looking decent, when she attached the string a tiny hint of breath escaped so that it shrank very slightly but was still capable of setting sail across the living room, a breeze from the window sent it up to the ceiling, a second breeze brought it back down to him, he handed his dictation to the teacher or rather handed him the balloon and the teacher had a red smudge on his cheek

—Cheke?

a couple of dogs lost interest in each other and wandered around the playground sniffing around for nonexistent rabbits or for the urine in the catheter bag, which seemed to excite them, as well as the slide there was a miniature merry-go-round, three wooden horses complete with manes, which had once been blonde and were now brown, the teacher wrote on the board, slowly and sensibly, *cheek,* he underlined *cheek,* drew an oval around it, enclosed the oval in a pentagon, underlining each letter twice, then hesitating

—Cheek?

uncertain

—Cheek?

silently shaking his head

—Cheek, my eye

then asking the doctor

—How do you spell *cheek?*

given that the blonde foreigner was English and, well, you know what English is like, the doctor taken by surprise

—Cheek?

trying it out on his notepad, then crossing it out, trying again in the margin

—Cheak?

then

—Oh, it doesn't matter

although the enigma remained as to why one eyebrow was thicker than the other, in that part of his memory where school days were clearest, not a male teacher but a female teacher adjusting her glasses with her middle finger, the diabetic student who had to inject himself in the middle of a lesson and who had problems with his glands and didn't have to get changed for gym lessons but sat on a bench, the name of that teacher suddenly leaped into his mind, Dona Anabela Sousa Ferreira, and he was astonished to find her so present, the musty smell of her jacket, her annoyance

—You must have copied from someone

the man's wristwatch that she held to her ear to make sure it was working, tapping the face with her little finger, unable to believe how long the classes lasted, how endless the nights were because the sleeping pills didn't work and her father kept nagging her

—How many years has it been since you visited my grave?

Dona Anabela Sousa Ferreira's hair dyed with cheap dye, bought not from a pharmacy but from a drugstore

—Do you have my usual hair dye, Senhor Medeiros?

the roots turning white, she would pause during the class

—Leave me alone, Dad

waving her pointer at him, then continuing the lesson,

the student who had problems with his glands always with the right answer, the mothers of his classmates to his mother

—Your boy seems a bit better

and his mother, who bought her hair dye from the same drugstore as Dona Anabela Sousa Ferreira, telling like rosary beads the X-rays, the tests, the spas

—A real burden

holding her son by the hand, him palely listening, the master of the times table and the grammar book, of adjectives, conjunctions and verbs, all the kings and queens in chronological order

—A real burden

he sometimes missed a week of school because his glands became overactive, and he would return looking still paler and with his ankles swollen, monotonously reeling off mountain ranges and battles, the headmaster to Dona Anabela Sousa Ferreira

—And to think what he might have become

and they both stood there frowning in melancholy fashion imagining him a government minister, the doctor forgetting about the chestnut for a moment

—If the boy with glands were here now he would solve the problem of how to spell *cheek* just like that

but one lurch of the adrenal glands and the cheek remained forever a mystery, a longing for the mountains brought back the abandoned trains and a locomotive that lay toppled onto its side in a pose like that of a dying animal, almost complete with snout, legs and a motionless tail, his grandfather opening the newspaper in the shade on the balcony, the curate's housekeeper cutting a bunch of grapes from the trellis, and silence because Dona Irene was absent and her harp slowly disintegrating in the cellar, who am I, Mom, guess, just as he could guess her answer

—I don't know

and her eyelids, not her eyes, looking for me, the doctor in a low voice, not a grown-up's voice, a child's, full of child-like surprise and terror

—Dona Anabela Sousa Ferreira had the same problem as you, you know,

the same problem, the same jacket, the same father nagging her

—How many years has it been since you visited my grave?

they get an idea in their head and never let it go, tormenting the living, Dona Anabela Sousa Ferreira not saying

—You must have copied from someone

as she did back then, eyeing her watch suspiciously, well, who can possibly understand time, Dona Anabela Sousa Ferreira a small flame flaring up, then burning out

—Is it dangerous, Doctor?

and dozens of balloons from Victoria's For Everything the Modern Woman Needs bobbing about in the hospital office, brushing against the desk, the filing cabinet, the couch, it wasn't just her roots that were white, it was half of her now-graying hair, whether because the dye didn't work or because she had stopped buying it at the drugstore, what was the point, and he too could ask

—What was the point?

why all the screens, the oxygen, the diapers, don't take the chocolate mice out of the little plastic cups, don't make me eat them in a glimmer of hope, the matter of cheek, cheak, cheke, chique remaining insoluble until the end of time, the doctor

—The same problem as you, you know

or rather the bicycle approaching the granite pillar and Dona Anabela Sousa Ferreira unable to turn the handlebars to avoid it, Dona Anabela Sousa Ferreira

—Is it dangerous?

and the doctor seated at the school desk hesitating before replying, the boy with the glands replying instead, he didn't complain, he didn't protest, he just clung to his mother, capable of listing adjectives, dynasties and conquests, which may well all now be under the ground feeding the worms, no slide at the doctor's school, a concrete playground where the puddles lasted all year, a map like his, the crucifix, the slate, the diabetic looking for his syringe and his name in turn jumping about, really, my memory, then the doctor triumphant

—Amadeu das Neves Pacheco

the stuff we drag around with us, dear God, what shall I do with Amadeu das Neves Pacheco, expel him or allow him to remain submerged along with other old names and other long-gone events, the doctor putting him away

—Amadeu das Neves Pacheco

in a private chest, getting rid of him, put him over there next to Dona Anabela Sousa Ferreira, her hair undyed and apparently with no idea who he was

—Is it dangerous?

too busy listening to her own innards, disappointed with them

—Why did you betray me?

Not that any of them responded

—I didn't do it on purpose, Senhora

just as the doctor breaks his chalk on the blackboard

—I didn't do it on purpose, Senhora

trying to put the pieces together and praying they would fit but they wouldn't, put the chalk in the chest too, show me how to deal with the past, and now how to deal with this tooth that's throbbing, an unexpected little heart inside my tooth beating away, I thought the tooth was just bone and yet it's alive, it shrinks and grows as it throbs away, no point calling for help, sheer torment, what happened to Victoria's For Everything the Modern Woman Needs, where his mother bought him a backpack, not the one he wanted but one with cloth straps rather than leather ones, during the whole of the first period he hated his mother for that

—Is it dangerous?

and of course it's dangerous, Dona Anabela, it will go on for five or six months, don't spend any more money on hair dye, you have quite enough in the bottle, don't worry, Dona Anabela Sousa Ferreira wasn't thrilled by the thought of saving money, when she arrived home she threw the bottle in the trash can in the kitchen, where the cancer-free canary sat in its wicker cage, not a male canary, because he didn't sing, a female canary with a haunted look in her eyes, according to the doctor's calculations Dona Anabela Sousa Ferreira was seventy-something, none of the cups match because things break, nothing lasts forever and she too remains unmatched, other people's sun on the curtains, other people's June and then on top of that this illness, what bad luck, hay fever, the air comes in but doesn't leave, just as the illness comes in and doesn't leave and that tooth throbbing ever harder isn't leaving either, the doctor's wife

—What a lot of fuss about a tooth

occupied simultaneously with a magazine and the oven, asking

—How do you write *cheek?*

and the wife, wearing a cheap blouse and a rather grubby apron, rising up from the magazine and from the oven

—Are you mad or what?

perhaps he was mad, brought to life by a child's chekes, spoken out loud

—Brought to life by a child's chekes

the doctor, who had never been in the mountains surrounded by empty trains that passed without stopping, and his wife staring at him in amazement

—I'm sorry?

not noticing the diabetic boy, the one who had problems with his glands, or Dona Anabela Sousa Ferreira announcing

—Dictation

following the lines with her pencil

—Title "The balloon"

everything so very present, the smell of her jacket, the watch pressed to her ear to make sure it was working, unable to believe how long the lessons were, how long the days, the nights eternal because the sleeping pills didn't work, her father nagging her

—How many years has it been since you visited my grave?

Dona Anabela Sousa Ferreira freeing herself from her father

—Is it dangerous?

time was such an impossible thing to understand, and she had so little time, five or six months at most, don't waste money on hair dye, what you have left in the bottle will be quite enough, and Dona Anabela Sousa Ferreira not over-joyed with the saving, Dona Anabela Sousa Ferreira before she arrives home throwing the bottle in the trash

—New line Brought to life by a child's cheeks

the canary in its wicker cage, none of the cups matched because things do break and nothing lasts forever and she too remains unmatched, other people's sun on the curtains, other people's June and on top of that the illness, a dozen balloons from Victoria's For Everything the Modern Woman Needs rising and falling, their strings waving good-bye.

25 March 2007

He could see faces but couldn't recognize anyone, people spoke to him but he wasn't listening, they were looking after him and yet it wasn't him they were looking after, the name he thought was his was a stranger's name, the body they were dealing with someone else's, he simply wasn't there and whose were those legs with no strength in them and those arms unable to make a single gesture, they kept asking him how he was feeling and he said nothing, incapable of responding

—It's not me they're asking

the stain on the shoe

—There's a little inflammation of the kidney we need to sort out

and what a strangely overfamiliar way to refer to something that lives under the protection of the skin, kidneys, lungs, pancreas busy with tasks that had nothing to do with him and that he imagined to be mere matter, and at this point his grandfather opened his own mouth as he held out the spoon to him and their teeth were identical except that his grandfather's were bigger, as big as his would be one day, the hygienist

—I don't like the look of them

whereas he quite liked them, they'd lived together for as long as he could remember, but as for his kidneys, lungs and pancreas, he had no idea what they were like and only a vague notion of what they were for, they came into existence gradually and then immediately went wrong, and on the table, beside the knives and forks of his grandparents and his uncle, were packages intended to moderate their mood swings, perhaps one grew bigger in order to make room for these precarious objects requiring injections and special diets, why on earth did age stockpile these terrible mysteries in people, the owner of the Englishmen's hotel grappling with his liver, Dona Irene refusing a cookie in the name of diabetes, he believed that people lived with him just as he lived with them and he was gradually discovering the incomprehensible substances they were made of and that he was also made of

—There's a little inflammation of the kidney we need to sort out

and that were, in the end, identical to all the others, full of little worms that were born after him and which, as well as occupying him, were themselves dying, he imagined death as a cortege of boots marching down the street rather than being a matter that concerned only the owner of the hotel and his liver, and this thought added to his feeling of surprise and terror because he was the only one dying, not the bramble-lined path or the source of the Mondego, but how to live with no hiding place, without even the eucalyptuses, the solitude of the end and the loss of the miserable little treasures he had stashed away

—New line Brought to life by a boy's cheeks

surrounded by a screen and yet despite the screen he

was still obsessing about those cheeks, nurses coming in and out, voices, orders being given, then fewer and fewer nurses, fewer voices, fewer orders, and his body in the hospital basement with the unplastered walls, a drawer opening and inside it the last balloon from Victoria's For Everything the Modern Woman Needs along with his childhood, the village with no chickens and no people, half a dozen old ladies going from alleyway to alleyway and one of those birds that become disoriented by the mountain mists in October only to be set on the right path again in April thanks to the kindly wind, what does a little inflammation of the kidney mean, what does illness mean, what is happening to me, the granite pillar again and me pedaling straight for it, what could my grandmother do besides say prayers and make jam

—Have a teaspoonful of this and you'll feel better

pointing at the trains she'd never actually traveled on, she'd never seen Lisbon, she'd never seen the sea, she lifted the piano lid, then closed it again because she was still in mourning for a brother-in-law who died of a fever in Goa and for whose body she was still waiting, the stationmaster

—I'll let you know as soon as the coffin arrives

found her on the platform, prayer book clutched to her breast and wearing a hopeful smile, how could you wait for some old bones for so long, Grandma, it wasn't the brother-in-law or his moustache that she had so often told us about

—The moustache of an artist

whom they presented to her in a box, but a few lumps of charcoal chosen at random and belonging to who knows who, his grandmother

—My brother-in-law was much bigger than this

rattling them about suspiciously, his mother rattling them too and saying

—India does tend to shrink corpses, Mom

my grandmother unconvinced

—Only last week your godfather turned up absolutely furious because his photo had been placed in the back row on the table

changing the order of the picture frames in a game of diplomatic precedence, the dead really care about hierarchies, you know, ambitions, prerogatives, vanities, you can't see my ugly mug unless you turn on the light, someone's taken a dress out of my closet, you never did wear that brooch I left you and don't go telling me you lost it, cousin Eufémia, cousin Galhó, great-grandfather Themudo, who dealt in hardware, invoices with Themudo & Sereno printed in the shape of a rainbow and underneath scribbled in pencil three locks and a price, whole heaps of the departed desperate for respect and him in the drawer without being told where his place was in the album or what kind of gravestone he was entitled to, he thought he could hear the ivy sighing at night or the chestnut trees giving up without our knowing because the leaves were still green and the chestnuts still growing, why did they hide their soul, Virgílio still saying

—I'm fine

shrinking to nothing on the pillow, a little drop of wine cheered him, brought some color to his cheeks

—I'll get up this afternoon

then he stayed in bed

—My legs won't do as they're told

his body almost invisible under the blankets, blocks

of unused invoices from great-grandfather Themudo and boxes of padlocks in the garage, boxes that had to be opened with a crowbar, and all sorts of other rusty old junk, great-grandfather Themudo on the shelf in the corridor where our minor ancestors gathered in cheap oval frames and yet the rainbow of names, Themudo & Sereno, remained imposing, there were July afternoons when the rain had stopped and you could see Themudo & Sereno up among the clouds above the ash trees, his grandmother

—It was my brother who paid off his debts

and his great-grandfather's glasses would get upset then, when anyone asked him about Senhor Sereno, he would shrug him off with a scornful look

—Sereno, huh

with furious disdain

—He took all the money he could possibly make off with

leaving the invoices as a souvenir, what did they do with their lives, dear God, bamboo walking sticks, satin collars, ringlets hiding their faces, his own grandmother with her hair in ringlets, sitting on the knees of a bald old man, and all of them now voiceless bits of charcoal in a box, he could see faces but couldn't recognize anyone, they spoke to him but he wasn't listening, they were looking after him and yet it wasn't him they were looking after

—It seems your kidney has recovered

and what did he care about his kidney, what is a kidney, how many relatives do I have now, relatives he didn't even know, pressing his nose against their bellies at his grand-mother's funeral

—Antoninho

creatures swallowed up by the fast train, lunch pack on

their laps, and once they left he never saw them again, his grandfather not reading his newspaper, his eyes gliding over the pages to the far side of the mountains, everything around him being turned into granite, even the sounds, he thinks he can hear footsteps when there are none, screams when there is silence, the railcars from the mine rattling silently along and the infection in his kidney saying nothing, only his father next to the source of the Mondego

—You know

when there was nothing to know, he didn't live in the village, he lived in a grave among the dead and the old ladies, just as today he was living in a white room in the rain while the nurse ordered him

—Go to sleep

but how could he go to sleep when he had seen what was in his diaper, how long did he spend studying his hands trying to work out how many nails and fingers he had, his grandfather's eyes fixed on him measuring him, his father on the verge of some decisive revelation

—You know

then immediately falling silent and him wondering what they were hiding, take me with you to walk beside the rivers, don't just leave me like this, the owner of the Englishmen's hotel feeling his neck

—This is a battle, my friend

and what was the hotel owner doing there if there was no more tungsten, no water in the swimming pool, the kitchen empty, sheep wandering randomly about in the scrub and the mountains growing taller, it'll be October in a few months' time and the wolves will be outside the school, who will toll the bell for him and accompany him to the family grave and those accumulated ashes that have lost their names behind the railings, the uncle who taught him to ride a bike

—Do you remember me?

I remember that he never married, he would go to the city and return looking very serious, refusing any lunch

—I'm not hungry

his grandmother uncomprehending

—Are you ill?

and his uncle underneath the ash trees prodding a frog with a stick

—I'm not a real man

he found him in the barn taking down a piece of rope from a hook

—I don't have the courage, lad

he left one day on the train

—I've found a job in Spain

and there was no Christmas card, the number of times he went down to the station of an afternoon to look for him among the passengers arriving or hoped he would open the door to his bedroom saying

—It's me

he thought he saw him on the road into town, crouched on a rock, kicking at the twigs with the tip of his shoe, he heard his footsteps around the house in January, he wiped the condensation from the window with the curtain but no one was there, the bicycle no longer able to perform figure eights relegated to the back of the pantry, he would run his fingers over the granite pillar

—Uncle

and still he didn't come back, he thought he'd spotted him in the hospital when they were carrying him along on a stretcher after an examination during which he and the illness

—I won't be leaving here

kept painfully filling up and emptying out, every cell a small suffering mouth, every nerve a gentle shudder, his uncle taking down the rope

—I don't have the courage, lad

not as he must have been like years later but as he was before, coming in through the gate in his Sunday best and him watching silently, months before a laborer hanged himself on that same hook, saying

—Antoninho

his tongue lolling, long, interminable, the cook tugging at his sleeve

—Quick, run

one boot on the ground, one boot on his foot, and still he didn't move, rooted to the spot, the rafters in the barn full of pigeons, sparrows pecking at a cartridge, mornings when he and his uncle would go into the pine forest, questions he wanted to ask but couldn't because he felt too embarrassed, fingers touching his hair, then immediately drawing back

—I hope you

his grandfather putting away his glasses and shortly afterward there were footsteps in the vineyard, Virgílio cut the rope with a sickle, they laid the laborer down in the cart, the mule turning its head to look, the cook in the hospital

—Quick, run

and there he was unable to get out of bed, they changed his sheets, rolling him first to the right, then to the left, his heart like the mechanism of the clockwork elephant that always fell out when dropped, the cart carrying the laborer moved off while he followed with his eyes the clouds over the mountains sliding eastward according to the whims of July, there was a village, and another one, which, when he drove through them with his father, were deserted apart from the occasional bonfire, some ragged cloths hung out to dry and a little goat tethered to a post bleating, why did they hide from them, who are they, his grandfather would have been able to tell him if he were capable of talking but his mother

—Leave him be

he lived besieged by fears no one would explain to him and he would die not knowing, the curate's housekeeper offering him a bunch of grapes from the trellis

—Don't you realize that none of us exists?

and if none of us exists, who was he and who had he grown up with, they visited him in the hospital bearing gifts he never touched, they raised the head of his bed and it wasn't the window he saw, it was boots and more boots at the gate, the oak trees peering over the wall of the viscount's garden and his father

—You know

even though his father was already dead and his mother

—Who are you?

touching his face with her fingers, how do you write *cheek,* Mom, and with the balloons from Victoria's For Everything the Modern Woman Needs between them, Dona Irene

—Would you like me to teach you a waltz, Antoninho?

she lived next to the pharmacy and went in and out of her house as quickly as the cuckoo in a cuckoo clock pressed for time, I remember Dona Irene's stepfather feeling his

way across the marketplace with the antennae of his walking sticks, Dona Irene's mother in the nursing home

—I think my asthma has improved, Doctor

but it hadn't

—We're going to add an antibiotic to the drip

and him not caring if they did or not, drips trembling,
falling, dissolving, none of us exists, not even the illness, the
hospital chaplain wearing a cross on his lapel

—Is there anything you want to confess?

but confess what, if there were no pine trees, no mountains, the granite pillar was getting closer, forcing him to
pedal faster, and so much mystery all around, Virgílio

—I'll get up this afternoon

but staying in bed

—My legs won't do as they're told

just as his legs wouldn't do as they were told either, before the operation, waiting to see the cancer specialist, silent people waiting, the workers from the tungsten mine
perhaps, going along by the river too

—Quick, run, Antoninho

and Antoninho running over the surface of the water all
mixed up with mud and twigs, he noticed the old ladies and
a gypsy encampment with the remains of bonfires while the
curate's housekeeper kept insisting

—Don't you see that none of us exists?

and he couldn't make out the trellis, he could make out
other, smaller villages, an unknown doctor agreeing with
the stain on the shoe

—It's possible

while he was running over the water that was lighter

than the mud and the leaves so clear in every detail, veins, stems, patches of brown

—Go and fetch the cart

but no sound of creaking hinges or wooden planks, the teacher saying only

—Brought to life by a child's cheeks

and him struggling with cheeks, chekes, chiques, cheaks, a child's cheeks bringing him to life, plumping him up, making him bigger but weightless, brushing against a wall, then spinning away from it, performing figure eights around the chestnut tree and the bicycle bell tinkling with pride, open the gate, Uncle, so I can pedal down the avenue and then if the doctors do bring the cart they won't find me in the hospital, Virgílio

—How's the boy?

and nothing but the bed and the machines, rain on the windows but not for him, possibly for you, not March, August, tomorrow and Thursday the wine harvest, his grandmother taking another straw hat down from the hat stand

—You're not going out in this sun without a hat

and it was, alas, a girl's hat with a pink ribbon, why not a beret, a cap, *cheak,* it's written *cheak,* a male thing and the teacher not striking out that *cheak* in red

—I'll let you off this time

the unknown doctor

—Ask the intern what he thinks

and why ask the intern if there are no mistakes in the dictation, *cheak* ruling supreme, I did it, it's obvious that the intern

—You're better

and the cart coming down the corridor in the direction

of the courtyard, a potato on the ground, rattling wooden planks, brambles on both sides of the path, Virgílio letting him hold the reins for a moment

—Right, that's enough

afraid that the wheel might go into a ditch and buckle the axle, his grandfather getting up from his newspaper and coming over to him and if he did that the trains would start running again, the mail train, the freight train, the fast train, not a single carriage on a branch line, not a single engine decaying in a siding, the stain on the shoe following a line

—I don't understand why he has a temperature

the mail train, the freight train, the fast train, the ones that pierced the night made up of shadows and windows, the station clock that was always slow moved one hand and it was actually right, his whole life was right, his clothes within reach in the closet, no need to whisper

—You know

Dad, because I know, if you know how to spell *cheek,* you know everything, better warn the curate's housekeeper

—Don't come telling me that none of us exists

that in a few minutes I'll be in Spain with my uncle, maybe I'll write at Christmas, I haven't really thought about it, perhaps I'll come back to the mountains or visit you and the gypsies still serious and silent, the stain on the shoe

—A problem, but where?

and the doctor he didn't know made a vague, all-embracing gesture indicating the whole of his body, by the source of the Mondego butterflies emerging from the moss, why don't you come walking along by the river with me, Dad, why do you keep looking at me, I can't hear you above the buzzing of insects, the stain on the shoe

—Pneumonia?

and the teacher saying

—Dictation

the teacher

—New line, title "Pneumonia"

pneumonia, pnewmonia, pneumoania and him remembering the little room where his grandfather used to go and shave, standing in front of a small mirror, one side of which was flat, the other concave, on the flat side you looked perfectly normal, on the concave side the hairs on your eyebrows were gigantic, his grandfather would scrape away at his neck with the razor, altering the shape of his mouth so as to tighten the skin, while he would stand there in the door filled with envy, the doctor swabbed a place near his ribs

—Sharp scratch

a sharp scratch my eye, the pain was so intense he became suddenly aware of every tooth in his head, incisors, eyeteeth, premolars, molars, seventeen terrible teeth, twenty-six, thirty-nine, and the surprise and the terror, a voice in his head saying very clearly

—I've died

and the liquid filling the syringe that his grandfather didn't even notice as he dried his razor on the towel and left the room buttoning up his shirt, the teacher

—I said buttoning up his shirt

while he was walking along by the rivers stubbing a toe on a rock, lingering in a puddle, stumbling onward, his grandmother pointing him out to the family

—Is that Antoninho?

and even had he wanted to reply what could he say to her except what the curate's housekeeper kept repeating

—Can't you see that none of us exists?

and his uncle wrapping the rope around his arm

—I didn't have the courage, lad

leaving the bicycle leaning against the garage door and setting off along the avenue of elm trees without a backward glance.

26 March 2007

There was a face missing and it wasn't his, since he could see it on his pillow, not yesterday's face, by which he would be known in the village, but today's face, by which he would be known in the ward, and therefore not the Antoninho he had lost but the Senhor Antunes he had gained there, incapable of riding a bike or strolling in the vineyard and with not a thought for the bicycle or the vineyard, if anyone should mention

—The mountains

he would spend a while pondering what they meant by *mountains* and he would forget just as he was forgetting what happened yesterday or what's happening right now, the clip on his forefinger tracking his heart's effusions on the screen, he imagined a fist pressing against his ribs and then a monotonous speech written in a strange calligraphy, each part of him a different language, all of them incomprehensible, the fact that there were so many alarmed him, as did the thought that there could be so much frenzied activity in one body and how so many languages could fit into such a small space, which one was the voice of the illness he couldn't find, he was trying to imagine his death but couldn't nor what it would feel like, he tried to hold on to the village with the old ladies and the caves but it slipped away, or rather he held on to just one old lady making noises like an ash tree stirring, perhaps that was death, a hidden potato, a face was missing and he couldn't find it, he found a lady telling the beads on her rosary but not praying, he stared at her and however hard he looked he couldn't recall her name, he tried Emília, Georgina, Ester, but neither Emília nor Georgina nor Ester fit, a name like that of the barber's wife, Hildebranda, there was a book on the shelf bearing an old-fashioned signature with the name Gracinda Borges Thomé, about a fairy called Hildebranda, he couldn't remember the story, but he remembered the magic wand with a star on its tip, all magic wands had stars on the tip and all stars were surrounded by rays of light, as he fell asleep Hildebranda

—Antoninho

and he started awake, frightened

—Don't come any closer

the cook too, how strange memory is, taking from him a box rattling with sounds

—If you play with matches you'll pee in your bed

in the cook's bedroom a doll with only one eye and the boots made to accompany funerals, boots filled with miles of misfortunes, perhaps he only had one eye too, because half the ceiling was blurred, he asked what the doll was called and the cook

—On Sundays she's Aurélia and the rest of the week she's Suzete

the nurse changed his position in bed and he noticed a knee grown suddenly scrawny and a bandage on his stomach made for a bigger man than him and therefore not for the Antoninho who is still in the village, at the mercy of the rooks yelling at him from above, he decided

—That knee doesn't belong to me

and yet he could bend it, the nurse giving him some juice in a glass

—I'll hold it for you, Senhor Antunes

and as always happens when someone else holds a glass to your lips, the rim was either too steep or too straight and it dribbled down his chin, his ailing grandfather

—What's the date today, children?

he who never spoke, besides his grandfather didn't say

—What's the date today, children?

his grandfather said

—I'm afraid

his grandfather said

—Be sure I don't

and the vineyard now dark red now green, what is the vineyard doing still down there while we're all feeling afraid because the world doesn't change at the same rate we do and what *is* the date today, seventh, sixteenth, twenty-first, not to mention the time, not that we care what time it is, dusk and dawn are identical, namely a kind of curdled half-darkness in which a face was missing but not his face, he made an effort

—What face?

and the lady with the rosary miscounting her beads

—I'm sorry?

as if what he had said were decisive, his grandfather

—What's the date today, children?

he in an attempt to help him although not at all sure he was right

—The eleventh

and his grandfather

—The eleventh

possibly relieved

—Thank heavens, the eleventh

and where is God if he doesn't even bother with us, his grandfather tentatively

—Are you sure it's the eleventh?

the chestnut trees that didn't care about numbers keeping up an endless chatter, the wind stirring them, the dense earth, at night their trunks

—When will it be morning?

and he from the depths of his bed

—I don't know, I'm only little

convinced that his uncle or Dona Irene would know, he knew about lizards and the names of provincial capitals but not about life, his clothes were too tight and his mother kept telling him off because his buttons wouldn't do up

—You keep growing

if he didn't stop growing, his straw hat would end up perched on top of his head, he didn't shave off the first absurd, stiff, black bristle of beard as he gazed into that mirror flat on one side and concave on the other, he snipped it off with some sewing scissors, holding the hair between two fingers, a few pimples, hitherto somnambular and now growing fragments inside his boxer shorts, what's happening to me, his uncle helped him onto the saddle of his bike and the pedals felt tiny beneath his feet, he looked at the cook's breasts differently now, he was filled with a strange feeling when he hugged her and then felt guilty, he eyed the peasant women furtively, alarmed at himself

—What's happening?

one Tuesday he found his father in the pantry, his back to him, embracing the maid, thrusting back and forth among the shelves full of packets and bottles, just like the pump in the well, and while the packets and bottles shook, the maid

—Aren't you ever going to come, sir?

a packet of salt toppled over, he would never forget the nailless toe on her slipperless foot nor her hairpins slipping out, the maid

—Look, sir, your son's watching us

his father becoming a blur of thrusts and then as he recovered he managed to utter words where before he had uttered only sighs

—My son?

walking past him in silence gathering up the last pieces of himself, the shirt he recognized and dark stains below his belt impossible to decipher, they never went back to the source of the Mondego, he never again heard his father say

—You know

he would observe him at the table feeling that his father was in turn observing him

—That's not my father

they could no longer be friends, nor could he feel proud when his father won at tennis and the look on the faces of the foreign women staying at the Englishmen's hotel resembled that of the maid, although their toenails were of course perfect, his mother another maid at night in the bedroom, and the ash trees

—Your mother

and his growing indignation, his father would pick up the tennis balls himself now, always looking for them in the wrong place, they didn't go down the Mondego together, they walked from rock to rock separated from each other, his mother looking up from her crochet

—What's going on between you and your father?

a packet of salt bursting open on the floor and him

—Nothing

like now with every bodily organ scribbling away for fear they might not finish what they wanted to say, reminding him of the trees in autumn, when they lose their leaves until they are nothing but bare branches, the room he was in detached from the neighboring rooms, alone, his grandfather

—What's the date today, children?

in the hope of being given a number and with that number an illusion of life, as long as there are numbers I'm still here, like me not in March but in August with the windows covered in black drapes so that death would not come calling, he looks more closely and sees a child in a corner and picks her up, there are fewer and fewer of us, half a dozen at most, and something or other was pulsating, quite what he didn't know, it couldn't be the well, because the pump wasn't working, nor was it the cart limping down the road, the Englishmen's hotel empty, the ailing tungsten miners on benches in the caves, the portrait of his grandfather arm in arm with his sister, both in their Sunday best, and, with the opaque eyes of someone who died a long time ago, ah, Aunt Luísa, he cheered up then and the memory of her name excited him because it meant that the mechanisms in his head were still intact, the stain on the shoe is sure to make me better

—Let's see

and that unenthusiastic

—Let's see

lacked a face and the mouth speaking independently

—There's a face missing

the one he always expected and that is sure to return suddenly comes back

—Antoninho

not even while he was ill did his father say

—You know

and the sun making the brambles by the clinic wall tremble, he considered taking his father's hand but the scene in
the pantry resurfaced and he didn't move, his father with
collar all twisted and a tube in his arm, say

—You know

loudly enough for me to hear, just say

—Child

and I'll come, the doctor

—He doesn't know you're there

but of course he does, he was showing me animal tracks
on the ground

—Look, you can tell a wolf's been here

in November a female wolf trotting through the corn-
field, a face was missing and he couldn't find it, what was it
that you never told me, the wolf distracted, what was it you
wanted to say but never did, his mother

—Your father

and then went back to her crocheting, so many secrets
and so much unfinished business, we don't talk in the village, we keep quiet, the curate in the church used to sing
about the glory of God, who wasn't there on the altar, per-

haps he was in town, where the people do him full justice instead of burying themselves in caves with their shawls and their forgotten potatoes like manna from heaven, the curate's hesitant Latin petering out and the bell sending the crows scattering, I tried

—You know, Dad

but he couldn't hear, I peered into the well and there was only mud at the bottom, as I peered into my father there was a void where the maid's words still echoed

—Aren't you ever going to come, sir?

and my father, who had indeed already come, looking very stern and dignified, he found the tennis racket and a couple of dusty balls, he didn't find the blonde foreigner on the edge of the swimming pool or the avenue of maples that led to the hotel, everything was beginning to fade and still the missing face did not come back, he remembered his grandmother in the morning waiting for the engine inside her to start, the village swathed in the vast folds of the mountains and the absence of trains making the distances greater, the bus would arrive with no passengers and leave with no passengers, he thought he saw the missing face, not Antoninho's nor that of Senhor Antunes, the one he needed in order to get better and leave that hospital bed, the nurse pushed him back against the pillow

—Don't get up

and perhaps the face is there on the bus disappearing off round the bend where the pine forest begins, does Dona Irene exist, does the harp exist or only the wind and what's left of the tungsten, he seemed to see his grandfather among the loquat trees, he called to him, but in the orchard nothing stirred, there wasn't even the smell of the hospital, a serenity that made him lighter, allowing him to float in the jelly of his illness, with pain keeping watch from beneath the medication and him a creature down a hole with the weasels waiting, the curate's housekeeper busy with the washing line strung between the elm tree and the pond, a face is missing, not his, Dona Lucrécia

—Boy

and him wanting to go and hide among the new vine growing up around the porch, where are the people who used to care about me, perhaps the cart will come back even if there is no cart, if I were to say

—Virgílio

I would be all right, Virgílio would be having his lunch alone in the garden, his bowl fenced in by his elbows, his knife at the ready to defend his food, there would be only the mountains, no trains, no village, no him, and he began to wonder whether the doctors were real and the nurses too, was he awake or asleep thinking he was awake, if he was in the same place as his grandfather he didn't care

—What's the date today?

given that every day is just one day and therefore no day, count the days on your fingers because your grandfather can't hear and would be astonished when you reached

—Thirty?

just as he would be astonished by forty-two or eighty, the sun to the left or the right of the house and with the changing sun the changing color of the hills, his grandfather sent messages to who knows who, argued with them, sat down

—Well, I never

one hand resting limply on the other, what was the use of hands that size, when he was well and healthy he used to run one hand over his clean-shaven chin in a slow caress, and his grandmother would whisper, not because she was afraid his grandfather would hear but because she was in the habit of whispering in church

—Do you think he knows we're here?

the doctor holding X-rays up to the light from the window, where the evening rain was growing old

—Don't worry, we still have a few more cards up our sleeve

and him listening as if in a warm mist, feeling more surprised and more terrified than ever, he could hear the chickens with their rounded wings settling down to sleep and the maid saying to him, even though he had never touched her

—Aren't you ever going to come, sir

while the bottles in the pantry trembled, there was a face missing and it wasn't his face, a few more cards up his sleeve, what a lie, what's the date today and the correct answer was two hundred, he said

—Two hundred

and the doctor uncomprehending

—Two hundred?

perhaps he would have preferred forty-two or eighty, don't worry, a few more cards up our sleeve, but there are no more cards, Doctor, see how my body is giving up, my heart writing only in small print now

—Look, your son's watching us

his father becoming a blur of thrusts and then immediately recovering

—My son?

walking past him tucking the last pieces of himself into his trousers, they never went back to the source of the Mondego, stones and moss and a bright green frog among the reeds, he never again heard his father say

—You know

he would observe him at the table feeling that his father in turn was observing him

—That's not my father

they could no longer be friends, nor could he feel proud when he beat his father at tennis and the look on the faces of the foreign women staying at the Englishmen's hotel resembled that of the maid

—Don't worry, we still have a few cards up our sleeve

he was amazed that they did even though one of the machines had been turned off and the sentences on the other were stopping and starting, reminding him of mornings when the wind dropped and there were whole flocks of birds on the ground, why don't they just crush the chestnut between two stones, the cook

—All those chestnuts will give you bellyache, dear

the pharmacist gave him a bitter powder

—Drink this

powdery grains stuck to the side of the glass and there was a sort of muddy residue in the bottom, don't add any more water, Senhor Fróis, don't make me swallow it, the cook

—I warned you

holding him by the wrists, she didn't smell of vegetables or fried food, her body smelled of the earth, her neck of the earth, her chest of the earth, her hips of the earth, turning him into earth too, then Maria Lucinda smiled at him and no face was missing, thank God, him still lost in his mist believing what the doctor said

—Don't worry, we have more cards up our sleeve

and the cook didn't need to hold his wrists, he drank the stuff down without complaint

—No need to hold my wrists, I'll drink it

the chestnut shrank and no threat remained hovering in the room, look, the heart and that other thing and the pancreas are all working again, clear lines forming his name, not Antoninho or Senhor Antunes but the secret name that only Maria Lucinda knew, one that his grandparents and his parents would never have guessed, the uncle with the bike

—Do a nice figure eight

had no idea either, the pharmacist to the cook

—In a quarter of an hour he'll be fine

and he was fine already, he was walking along by the rivers, leaving behind the mountains and the villages, where a man, armed with a mallet, was making his way to the mouth of the river, no missing face now that Maria Lucinda has arrived, the nurse saying to a person he couldn't see, probably the lady with the rosary

—He's cheered up, hasn't he?

soon Dona Irene's harp and his grandfather's newspaper arriving on the noon train, his father

—You know

having forgotten all about the maid

—What were you going to tell me, Dad, don't disappear now

finding all the tennis balls in the bushes, the owner of the Englishmen's hotel

—What's the girl's name?

and he so timid, so proud

—Maria Lucinda

she lived between the hotel and the village, next to the

junction where a tractor was slowly falling to pieces, I'm not ill, I'm fine, we still have a few cards up our sleeve, Doctor, a small house, a tangerine tree growing by the wall and the tangerines so unbelievably orange, a cat that existed and didn't exist and when it didn't exist they

—The cat?

went looking for it, on Wednesdays his mother

—Where are you off to?

before disappearing into her crocheting again, I'm off down the rivers, Mom, or on the eleven o'clock freight train, the stain on the shoe

—Don't let him get out of bed

but how could they stop him if he was bounding up the little hill to her house, pleased because the cat existed again, rubbing against his legs, the other doctor

—His blood pressure's come down

and an old lady observing him with beady eyes, an aunt, a stepmother, some relative or other, he never dared to ask

—Who's that?

he kept very still, aware of Maria Lucinda's hair, for she lived alone, and around them the shifting smudge of crows coming and going, no missing faces now, they're all there, the curate, Virgílio, the gypsies with their knives not in their pockets but in their eyes and him in his own personal mist not attaching to anyone, if they tried to grab him he would dodge out of the way, the old woman saying nothing because peasants inhabit the silent side of the earth, what are they made of apart from boxwood and tungsten, all the faces were there with him, everything was ready, when he mentioned Maria Lucinda his grandmother

—Ah, the curate's daughter

why didn't she just leave on the first bus, why did she stay in the village, and Maria Lucinda

—I can't leave

because no one left, they came back just as he had when he was admitted to the hospital, he thought he was in Lisbon but he wasn't, I found myself standing next to you near what remained of the Englishmen's hotel, one day he caught her receiving a package from the curate's housekeeper, she let him sit under the tangerine tree, and what became of the chestnut he had lost and the pain that didn't bother him, in his mind

—I'm better

he was heading down those rivers on his way to the sea, his father finally

—You know

and there was no need for him to explain, he knew, all he needed was the certainty that he would reach the mouth of the river, his grandmother

—The fast train the mail train the freight train

and the newspapers at the station, his grandfather with one hand cupping his ear

—Can you hear the trains, child?

and yes, he could hear the trains in the siding beyond the vineyard and Maria Lucinda was there too, and him saying

—You didn't die, Dad

playing tennis at the Englishmen's hotel and him feeling proud of his father, I act as ball boy, and Maria Lucinda

—António

no

—António

no

—Senhor Antunes

and don't worry, we still have a few cards up our sleeve, the doctor saying

—He's gone to sleep

but he wasn't sleeping, just concentrating on the old lady wrapped in the shawl, his aunt, his stepmother, a relative of some sort with her hidden potato, he hadn't fallen asleep, he wouldn't fall asleep, he didn't want to sleep, he noticed his father's

—You know

and a bicycle doing figure eights between the chestnut tree and the gate, his uncle

—Faster

and Maria Lucinda

—António

the curate was leaving the church, rowing along the street with his walking stick, and Maria Lucinda touching his face with her hand, not the face in the hospital ward, the face from years before, his mother's voice

—Are you feeling better?

Maria Lucinda's hair merging with his and him slipping down the rivers to become one with the waves.

27 March 2007

The room didn't change, the lights remained the same, the nurses fussed around him at their usual pace saying the usual words, and yet still he had the feeling he was in the middle of quite what he didn't know, something on which his life depended but that had nothing to do with his illness and had grown so faded with the years that he couldn't find it, the key capable of unlocking the door that led to himself and to the stillness of peace, the same peace his grandfather felt when they offered him a spoonful of food and he said

—No

inhabiting a place where the cortege of boots could not follow him, dozens of vines to prune and piles of newspapers on the balcony and his grandfather indifferent to it all, so close to that quite-what-he-didn't-know and happy to be so close, the door that led to himself just within reach, he pushed it open and found himself there, a child playing with buttons and cotton reels, each button a living creature, each cotton reel a soul, a second door and the barking of the stray dog one of the laborers had poisoned, his father with his arm raised in order to strike the man only to lower it again without even touching him

—Get out

he remembered the laborer and his wife leaving the village with a goat and a little girl behind them, both tethered by a piece of string, daughter and goat, goat and girl taking tiny steps just like his uncle's two fingers, forefinger and middle finger, advancing over the tablecloth at lunchtime

—I'm coming to get you

and him shrinking back in his chair because his uncle's fingers were a monstrous insect about to tickle him, he tried to spear the insect with his fork and the insect turned into a furious hand suddenly regaining all its missing fingers, one of which was full of endless threats

—So you wanted to hurt me, did you?

and he hadn't wanted that at all, he was just afraid the insect would reach his knee or his belly with a cruel little laugh when even his uncle's eyes became teeth and inside the teeth of his eyes two fierce pupils, the girl, the goat and him starting to whimper and the forefinger and the middle finger dissolving into the cutlery

—Don't be such a sissy

a couple of men were cutting down the chestnut tree and if the tree died then he would die too but what did dying mean, grasshoppers died, chickens died, but people didn't, they were nailed into a box and spoke from within

—Have you seen my scissors?

just as the wooden chest said

—I'm full to bursting with clothes

and the raindrops from last winter in a hole in the roof

—I'm going to make you nice and wet

they placed saucepans underneath and sharp little sounds followed

—Here we come

he held out his thumb to receive a drop and the drop dodged him and fell elsewhere

—You missed

his grandmother indignant

—Leave the winter in peace

the logs in the hearth spat saliva as they burned, the world gray and the chests of drawers dressed in mourning, dozens of handkerchiefs emerging starched from a pocket and returning screwed up into a ball, a hand on his neck

—Do you have a temperature?

and his chest a jittery frying pan, blankets that smelled of musty trunks and the air full of right angles, there was neither too little nor too much of anything but it wasn't his bedroom, they had given him an identical one to fool him, he heard himself say in a strange sleepy voice

—Give me back my room

in place of the fallen chestnut tree a void, where am I going to do figure eights now, tell me that, the well won't do, not with all those drowned men at the bottom, when brought up to the surface they were a gigantic dripping bundle of hair and sleeves and underneath that feet that frightened him and the absence of any face, meanwhile his mother's nose pecking at him and armed with a terrifying glass of water

—Swallow the pill whole, don't chew it

the pill resisting, clinging with suckers to his throat and the sharp isosceles of the water hurting him

—Has it at least gone down?

inside him flesh and narrow tubes on fire, a feeling that he was dreaming and running at the same time, heat on the surface and waves of cold beneath, his mother's nose pitiless

—You must eat, just be patient

and the tubes, not him, refusing the soup, his uncle's fore-finger and middle finger advancing over the quilt

—I'm coming to get you

he couldn't defend himself with his arms because he had no arms, he had become a drop of water on the end of a piece of rope and his feet were capable only of walking through chasms of mud, his mother took a handkerchief out of her apron pocket

—I think you're having me on, you little rascal

he turned to the wall, where he saw a squashed mosquito he hadn't noticed before, not normal mosquito size but with huge feet and great bulging eyes, and there were flaws in the plaster that he hadn't noticed either and that the flu had revealed to him with the clarity of a microscopist, peeling paint, stains, the palm print left by the maid when she was changing the sheets, he placed his hand on top of it and it was smaller, he couldn't believe that he would one day cease to be a child and wear glasses, that he would cough and be listened to with respect

—Exactly

won over by the authority of his bronchitis, a newspa-per just for him, on which he commented with indignant circumspection

—What's all this about?

on redundancies and interest rates, the number of events he missed along the way astonished him, even in the hos-pital his uncle's finger continued to advance, implacable, terrifying

—I'm coming to get you

and he stayed quite still and unresisting, the suspicion that his uncle wasn't in Spain

—The mud was calling to me

and on the end of a rope a dripping bundle of clothes and hair, the laborers turning the wheel and his uncle jerking up to the surface, one of his shoes with the sole missing and a polka-dot sock he had never seen before, perhaps the drowned swap clothes, why don't you try this tie and I'll try those socks

—Whose socks were they, Uncle?

and a complicated response bubbling with detritus, he used to sit on the balcony feeling bored with himself

—Go away, boy

go on, Uncle, tickle me, I don't mind as long as you cheer up, I'll find you a beetle in a bottle, we can have a race backward and I'll lose, what do you think

—A beetle?

a beetle, a gecko, the present from last year's Christmas cracker, one of Snow White's dwarves with a ring in its cap so you could hang it on your lapel, when you go into town wearing that dwarf, people will be jealous, they will, honest, I am, his mother studying the dwarf

—Where did that ugly thing come from?

his uncle hesitating and in turn studying the dwarf

—Do you really think it's ugly?

pulverizing me with a cruel sideways glance, the mud in the bottom of the well calling to him

—Quick

and his uncle standing on the edge

—It's all your fault, Antoninho

a farewell he would never forget, that is, the forefinger and middle finger no longer advancing toward him but toward themselves, their body gone, the fingers continuing to walk, if you ever got too close they would set off obstinately, incorporeally, toward no one at all, they might one day reach the mountains

—I'm coming to get you

and disappear among the rocks, the number of memories lost over time and which he came upon now with a shock, the feeling that he was in the middle of quite what he didn't know, something on which his life depended but grown so worn and faded by the years that he couldn't find it, his father no longer making the shelves in the pantry rattle as he fiddled with his belt, putting his hand in his pocket that was still down by his ankles and handing the maid some money

—Please don't tell my wife

he had never come across an arm capable of reaching down through the floorboards to the cellar, where a mouse was trying to bite him, wrinkling its nose, with boxes and a gate at the far end, where there was a square of sky called Paradise in which souls exulted, outside the cellar the square was just a patch sewn onto the clouds, because you could see the thick thread, and the turtledoves sniffing the wind until they found the corridor of a breeze that would help them escape, his uncle's words of censure

—It's all your fault, Antoninho

and him filled with remorse

—I'm sorry

unable to find a beetle in a bottle or a dried frog that might cheer up his uncle, his father's arm drooping just as his nose and his eyes were drooping

—Please don't tell my wife

prowling round the well and throwing in a pebble which

took a while to touch bottom, his stepmother finding his father in the house with their next-door neighbor

—Bernardino

and Bernardino was written on the screen of his heart, the stain on the shoe saying to the nurse

—Do you see that, Bernardino?

trying to diagnose that endlessly repeating signature while his father was hunkering down in the bed looking for knees and elbows that could hide him, the wood lice curling up, the ants disappearing into the bricks, and yet the sheet didn't even cover his shoulder, look at that birthmark and the scar where a reed stuck in him, and beyond the heart, the liver and the lungs

—Bernardino

and perhaps his father was referring to his stepmother that day by the Mondego

—You know

staring at the dragonflies and not at him, how complicated life is, the neighbor took ages getting dressed, her blouse the wrong way round, a sandal she had to get down on all fours to find and which could be retrieved only with the handle of the mop, his stepmother

—How awfully kind of you

while the sandal went flip-flopping down the alley sniveling beneath the disapproving pine trees, perhaps the wolves from the school ate her up, approaching with forefinger and middle finger, the world bristling with forefingers and middle fingers that never forgot anyone, advancing slowly, first one, then the other, and however fast people ran they would always catch up to them, the only option was to become dripping bundles of hair and clothes in the redeeming waters of the well, the boots ready for a slow march that went straight past the cemetery and disappeared into the mountains among nameless trees, what happened to his father would happen to him, becoming a breath of cold north wind and there being no one left to look after the chickens and the rain in the living room, if you touched the shoulder of the curate's housekeeper she would almost jump out of her skin, then smile

—You're soon back, Antoninho

picking the bunch with the most golden grapes

—Try one, dear

worried about him

—You've lost weight in the hospital

noticing that his suit was too big and his shirt huge

—Didn't they treat you well?

they suck us dry with endless tests, they don't let us thrive, the bishop's car crossing the square kicking up dust and making the rooks cough, when he visited his mother instead of her asking

—Who are you?

she said mournfully from behind her blindness

—You never saw the bishop

and he never did see the bishop, others pointing out the arches

—His palace is still there

and an old lady dressed in black

—She was the one who used to do his ironing

hiding a potato underneath her shawl, if the doctors cured him and he went home he would find an arm feeling in pocket after pocket for coins

—Please don't tell my wife

and the maid smoothing her clothes, and you cutting such a pathetic figure, Dad, so contrite and fearful

—You know

and I don't know anything, none of us knows anything, my stepmother

—Bernardino

and the stain on the shoe following him on the screen

—His heartbeat's irregular

who is it who insists on plunking us down in the middle of quite what we don't know, something on which our life depends, so few answers to the questions we silently ask, we're all the same, and me in turn saying

—You know

while his father was waiting, don't expect answers, Dad, because we've both given up, there are still coat hangers in the closet, a kind of remorse and a kind of hope but hope for what

—Bernardino?

letters stashed away in a tin box, Aunt Alina died, cousin Jorge got married, a child drinking tea from a saucer, resting the saucer on his chin, another tuning the strings on a harp before beginning to play a melody, then immediately stopping

—I've lost my gift for music

trivial sins, faded joys, flowers in pots on the steps, the maid saying to my mother

—Your husband

and my mother continuing to beat the egg whites for the cake, the only occasion on which the bus had a passenger was that week when it carried off the maid, my mother moved into his room, bolting herself in behind silences, and he moved into the pantry among the jars of barley and chickpeas with the names written on labels in brown lettering still blue around the edges, his father alone in bed, stumbling through sleepless nights, his eyes in the morning having escaped his eyelids, one in the middle of his cheek and the other still adrift on one temple, finding each other again only at the door to the bedroom

—I swear I didn't do anything

and the nightdress emerged from beneath the sheets, brandishing a rosary

—Begone, Satan

disputes in the sacristy, confessions, penances, promises that the curate negotiated meanwhile anxious about a swelling on his ear while the sacristan was busy varnishing the images of the saints, the curate dabbing cautiously at his earlobe with a piece of cotton wool

—These problems always work themselves out eventually

finding precedents in the Gospels to appease my mother, and as for my father, he was beginning to get rather fond of the pantry and the ferment in the tins where the chickpeas were sprouting just as in the early morning you can feel your hair growing, because everything in us grows, not just our nails and the years, we should change our name as we expand, not just from Antoninho to Senhor Antunes but from Filipe to Sérgio or from Fernando to Jaime, becoming strangers to ourselves and living elsewhere, the nurse

—Are you talking to me, my friend?

and him without a word to say, what did he care about pain, malaise, sickness, visitors

—Here we are

but they weren't, they would grow accustomed to the

small void he would leave, as easy to fill as a moment of tedium at work or this ache in my back that hurts when I move, and yet despite everything I put up with it, his mother in the marital bedroom again and him missing the pantry so much that he decided to put a can of grain on the bookshelf, and my mother having forgotten all about the curate

—You've obviously turned out just like your father

looked at her rosary when she mentioned his father but left it there on the nail, and simply moved the pillows on the bed farther apart

—Don't you dare touch me

and my father's eyes set adrift again, the curate, turned arbitrator once more, gathering some spit in his mouth to clean a stain on his cassock

—Such a change of heart is an offense to God, my dear lady

and so the pillows moved half an inch nearer and my father's eyes calmed down, he tried to move his eyes around too, but they remained symmetrical, perhaps today in the ward one of them was resting on the window and the other on the ceiling, he could hear the elevators and someone laughing in the distance, he was in the middle of quite what he didn't know, something on which his life depended, but he couldn't find it, if he was tempted to mention this, one of his visitors

—Don't tire yourself

and into his mind came the image of the mule abandoned at the foot of the mountains pursued by animals it couldn't see, toothless apart from its incisors, the curate's teeth detached themselves from his gums, complicating his Latin, his uncle's forefinger and middle finger advancing over the altar, meaning to help, and the curate protecting himself with his cope, who isn't afraid of fingers coming inexorably, solemnly closer and closer

—I'm coming to get you

and ending up on your belly in a frenzy of tickling, the curate's teeth all higgledy-piggledy

—Leave us

the housekeeper found him in the afternoon in the chair by the trellis frenziedly counting the pine trees, when she arrived this frenzy only grew and his hat fell off and one of his legs was at an awkward angle, ash trees in the sunlight and the stain on the shoe deciphering the screen

—The priest in his village has died

because his whole story, not just the

—Bernardino

nor the

—Please don't tell my wife

was being written in his room, there were the child's cheeks that brought me to life and the

—Can't you hear the cat's tail twitching?

in the conch shell of the house, what was he thinking, what did he want, what was he hiding from the others, Maria Lucinda's hair, Maria Lucinda who lived alone, another woman he never mentioned, shrouded inside him like a secret light, and the stain on the shoe pondering the screen

—It's a woman's name, isn't it?

all the secrets of which he was composed on show to the visitors and the visitors amazed

—The lies he told us

and he wasn't lying, he kept silent, one knee bent

—Antoninho

and there was no Antoninho, there was a Senhor Antunes worrying about a chestnut and the medicines incapable of altering the meaning of the pain, he tugged at the reins of the mule and a little drop of urine, a little drop of dribble, the secret light flickering, him

—Don't leave

and the light continuing to shine purely out of pity, the curate's housekeeper lacking the courage to shake him by the shoulder

—Aren't you going to the seven o'clock service?

so that the curate could straighten his chasuble, asking

—Have I died?

checking that everything was in order so as not to offend death, legs, arms, the hooks on his cassock, but what do hooks prove, show me a dead man who doesn't take scrupulous care over his appearance, full of delicate gestures, if they find a loose thread on our collar, they remove it, they want us to be clean and decent so that they can proudly present us to their colleagues

—My nephew Antoninho

his mother's blind eyes observing what cannot be seen, a hidden bird, ghosts whose existence we deny but who still haunt us, what's happening in the village, what's happening to me, the chestnuts still tiny buds on the branches threatening to grow, the curate's housekeeper

—Don't you bother saying the rosary now?

and the curate didn't bother saying the rosary, twenty-seventh March and you sleepily boiling a kettle on the stove, wearing an old dressing gown you never used to wear when you were with me, the furrowed brow of someone struggling with what's left of the night and your cheeks gradually filling out, the house in the morning not yet a house because we bump up against the objects still looking for their places in the living room, the table becoming a table, the dahlias in the vases becoming flowers, Virgílio's cart transporting the curate to church, sitting like him on top of the potatoes, and the chair by the trellis empty, how lonely the world seems when chairs are empty and the shadows can't make up their minds

—Shall I sit on the chair or on the floor?

they try the chair, they try the floor, then give up, the curate's housekeeper clapped her hands in the hope that the shadows would sing like turtledoves but they don't, they're too busy thinking

—What shall we do?

when his mother had the dovecote taken down

—They leave their mess everywhere

the disoriented doves fluttering around the absence of perches, we reach the balcony and not a dove to be seen, feathers, droppings, a little egg in the grass, a toad swallowed the egg and became quite spherical, sticking out his elbows like a clerk behind a counter, you on the bench forgetting about your coffee while your features slowly took up their usual places and your hand scratched the back of your neck empty of ideas, Virgílio ran over a stone and the curate cheered up

—I didn't die, how funny

drove past the stone and the curate dead, behind the windows in the chapel the branch of an acacia tree more imposing than the altar, the doves did not return and his mother missed them, Virgílio turned the handle on the brake and the mule's ears followed, the room didn't change, the lights remained the same, the nurses fussed around him at their usual pace, saying the usual words, and yet still the feeling that he was in the middle of quite what he didn't know, he used to play with buttons and his mother's cotton reels, each button a living creature, each cotton reel a soul, when his grandmother put her thimble on and held a blouse closer to the lamp a feeling of eternity and happy sweetness, the curate's housekeeper

—Antoninho

given that nothing happened, the curate in the chair by the trellis, Virgílio's cart far off, the stain on the shoe

—Nothing happened, my friend

each organ writing its own name on the screen smoothly and unhurriedly, the nurse

—We're still here, my friend

and we really are, but why the old dressing gown when I'm here to keep you company, you hesitating with the furrowed brow of someone struggling with what remains of the night, the sight of your bare feet moved me, your little finger red and the others white, a piece of label stuck to your heel but you didn't notice, one hand, elbow raised, scratching the back of your neck, sheets on the washing line under the awning and a blouse soaking in a plastic bowl, and I feel, or felt, I say *felt* because the diapers they put on me at the hospital need changing, they have to lift my legs up and wash me and yet despite this you're here, sitting on the sofa after lunch, you with two cushions because of your hernia and me with no cushion and perhaps a hernia too or, no, a kind of ache, I like it when it rains on the hospital window, I like it when it rains on the awning while we're watching TV with no need to speak, your hand, not scratching your neck now but resting on my knee, and what a difference there is between a hand on the back of the neck and a hand on the knee, my trousers becoming skin and it's my skin, not the fabric, that you're stroking, occasionally your head on my shoulder, even more occasionally a kiss, I raise my head for a second kiss and the distant mouth says

—Are you enjoying the movie?

I haven't even noticed the movie

—Oh yes, hugely

how could I possibly notice the movie when someone's rubbing my buttocks, not a man but a female nurse humiliating me

—I won't be long

drying my private parts with swift efficiency, parts that aren't even that private anymore but ugly limp rags, I really am enjoying the movie, though, I promise, I just feel a little sad, don't worry, I'm not very sad, just a tiny bit, and I really don't want to bore you with such a tiny insignificant sadness, the thought that I won't see you again.

28 March 2007

He ceased being a person without even realizing it, he was a fish swimming in water far denser than the water that other people called air and that he also used to call air before the pain that wasn't exactly pain

—I promise you won't feel any pain

and because it wasn't exactly pain it bothered him all the more, he wanted his pain to be there, to feel alive through the suffering, and there he was, a fish that occasionally moved not an arm or a leg but a vague kind of fin, and when he opened his mouth nothing came out, the others

—What did he say?

and he hadn't said anything, only silent bubbles, and those bubbles were saying

—Give me my pain

and they were denying him the dignity of pain, on the water glittering lights dissolving and reforming only to dissolve again, for a moment he thought he must have drowned in the well and that the rope on the bucket would come and find him, but what was missing was the smell of the pine trees and the breeze from the mountains, pain crept over to have a look at him, then vanished without so much as touching him, there were other shapes in the water apart from him and the pain, the blonde foreigner from the swimming pool moving off, what should he call her, not that he knew her name, she was at most a hand waving as she walked away, as he tried to reach the surface, where the visitors were waiting, he remembered a friend of his grandfather's, Senhor Hélio, struggling up the steps one Sunday, raising one foot while clinging to the wall and conquering the first step, trembling with the effort, he wouldn't let anyone help him

—I must do this alone

his neck spilling out over his tie and his nostrils gaping, at Easter, in the middle of lunch, he toppled over like a chess piece onto his plate while his grandfather sat on the balcony beneath his dome of silence, and when his mother wrote to him with the news, he returned the piece of paper unread, giving it only a cursory glance, as he did with the newspaper, impassive, silent, almost on the surface of the water, where the lights gave way to people, when they lifted Senhor Hélio up off the tablecloth he was doubtless staring down at it just as he had stared down at the steps angrily weighing them up, and my mother lacked the courage to tear up the letter out of respect for the dead, many years later he found it in a drawer, written in pencil, in shaky capital letters, along with little bottles of nail varnish, gloves and an old door handle that didn't open living-room doors but a void into the void, how else could one write about death other than in shaky capital letters and his mother her soul full of bats, anyone who insists that the dead are not alive doesn't know the world, the letter must still be there among the ruins of the house and Senhor Hélio outside gathering strength for the next effort, the gypsies will have occupied the courtyard and the old ladies will have taken over the kitchen, a relative was squeezing his fingers

—Do you think he can understand?

but understand what, the pain, the blonde foreigner by the swimming pool, the now nonexistent stains, what existed were the words that were being whispered from behind someone's hand and that he couldn't hear, the curate took his rifle and went hunting in the mountains for rabbits, the children from the village didn't venture beyond the ash trees, fearful of the deserted villages and the tools hanging on the doors of the shacks, hoes, buckets, mats, suspicious of the curate because he returned intact with dead animals hanging from his belt, hang me from your belt too, Curate, and take me away from this hospital, stride down the corridors with me bumping against your thighs and hand me over to your housekeeper so that she can pluck me, at confession the curate would hurriedly cross himself as he went through the list of sins, greed, envy, sloth he could understand but what did *luxuria* mean

—What does *luxuria* mean?

his grandmother who was peeling apricots said she didn't know either, she knocked at my uncle's bolted door, his shoulders already dripping even before Spain and before the well, not interested in beetles and toads, look, here are Senhor Casimiro's candies, the sort that used to get stuck in your teeth and that you couldn't get out even with your fingernail

—Lend me your dictionary, will you?

she put it down next to the apricots, *luxuria,* endless pages of enigmatic words, *erythrocytosis, graminaceous, leveret, luxuria,* and his grandmother reading out loud the entry for *luxuria,* abundance, sumptuous delight, pleasure, vicious indulgence, sexual appetite, lasciviousness, concupiscence, excessive desire, passion, synonyms indecency and lubricity, antonyms, innocence, and he had repeated all this in the church, adding, just in case, graminaceous and leveret, the curate drowning beneath a torrent that was obstructing his reason

—Say one Hail Mary and be off with you

and as he left he heard the curate say

—Leveret

rabbits on his brain, twitching noses and legs like mattress springs, the Mondego reduced to a mere thread skirting round clods of earth, he waited for them outside their burrows and the shot he fired echoed from valley to valley, laying low the surrounding bushes spelling out

—Lasciviousness

—Concupiscence

—Passion

disorienting the rooks and crows flying up from the corn

—Excessive desire

then suddenly dropping down again surprised

—Excessive desire?

the person checking the IV drip in his arm to a colleague he couldn't see

—Can you get what the guy's saying?

as if anyone can get anything anyone says in this world, whenever he went back to confession, the curate would hurriedly make the sign of the cross and send him away again

—You're all ready for heaven, so off you go

his grandmother shouted to his uncle, too scared to pick up the dictionary just as she was too scared to pick up a scorpion

—Remove that monster from my kitchen

disoriented by all those thousands of words she'd never heard of, *artifact, diegesis, iconoclast, neonatology,* the universe far larger than she had imagined, full of things she didn't know about it, paraphernalia, for example, lurking in some corner of the house, jaws agape, there were probably iconoclasts and artifacts in the village, and what would she do if a diegesis

—Come over here

the room bristling with words, all of which had it in for her, every one of them, and there he was on the surface of some water that was denser than the water that other people called air and that he also used to call air, thinking about the pain they'd stolen from him, something or other, in the body of his body breaking on the morning beach that was definitely him, for there were no other human footprints, the first birds, the first flotsam, a smile

—Antoninho

but who and where, the woman who brought the milk, the wife of Senhor Casimiro, the contortionist from the International Traveling Circus found and lost at seventeen, everything he had once been was close to him now, his grandmother asked the maid to burn the dictionary on the stove, he thought he was inhabiting a morning identical to that morning beach, the sea pale in the distance, the foam purple, sparrows, no, there are no sparrows on the sea, albatrosses, no, not in the plural, a single albatross, its wings buoyed up on the sea breeze, or a red kite finding a partridge chick among the broom, the doctor

—First they get better, then they get worse and very gradually they waste away if only the red kite would carry him off on its wings, stuck to its feathers like a piece of earth, the maid holding up the dictionary

—It's too big for the stove

anyway, it seems luxuria is a gigantic sin, build a bonfire and burn the *diegesis* and the *iconoclast,* what's all that loud and light rustling in the eucalyptus trees, it's the angels sent by God to check up on our mistakes, in pictures they're shown playing trumpets, putting a halo around the head of Saint Mary of Egypt and fighting dragons, the pages of the dictionary now curled and ashen, the spine broke with a crack, he thought his uncle was watching from the window, but the curtain didn't move, I confess to the sin of luxuria, Father, and the curate not even listening and uttering a hasty blessing

—I thought I told you to leave

with the mountains full of waiting rabbits and now and then a wild boar trotting along on its tiny legs, wolves of whom the only trace was a disemboweled badger lying like him disemboweled in bed, who killed me when I arrived here and who continues to kill me, they return on the pretext of giving him some soup

—Just a few spoonfuls, Senhor Antunes

but they didn't open their mouth wide as his grandfather used to do, nor did they dangle chocolate mice before him, holding them by their string tails, how many days with this pain waiting to be a pain, deceiving me about the chestnuts, I can't even feel them but they're there, I'm a tree, you know, send two laborers to cut me down like they did the chestnut tree, a void the size of a ravine between the granite pillar and the house, we try to take a step and we fall, only I'm not quite sure where, there must be another side and on the other side the morning sea, rooks, ash trees, there are no rooks or ash trees in the sea, on the other side waves and a cradle in the sand, his uncle put his suitcase down on the quilt on his bed and started taking clothes out of the closet before setting off for Spain, these patients get better, then get worse and very gradually they fade away, nights spent staring at the window listening to the sounds of the hospital, the tinkle of a bell mingled with the sound of a faucet being turned on and the smile of his seventeen-year-old self cheering him on

—Come on, then

him fearfully buttoning up his coat

—I can't, I don't know how

and beyond the balcony a building with a limp flag attached to the top of the pole, the stain on the shoe pointing at the screen with his little finger

—There's a change in his heart rate

in a script incomprehensible to the doctor and comprehensible to him

—What shall I do now?

the cook buried the ashes of the dictionary in the wooden vat on the far side of the vineyard so as not to contaminate the vines, Senhor Hélio ages ago now standing on the third step shaking his head, when he dies they'll hand a piece of paper to his mother and she, incapable of deciphering it

—What's this?

it's nothing, Senhora, nothing happened, his father in his tennis gear

—Please don't tell my wife

he tried to say

—Dad

he asked

—Dad?

and he lost him, where have you gone, why aren't you sitting by my side

—You know

what was he trying to tell me, an arpeggio from Dona Irene, the stain on the shoe

—He's a lot better

and since I am better I should make the most of it, even if I drown in the water denser than water I can still hear you, the doctor talking more to himself than to the others

—Sometimes these things

the oxygen level reducing because a red arrow moves from thirty down to twenty, the pain made as if to begin but stopped to consider, shall I hurt him or shall I not, then it withdrew and now, yes, he found he could speak, he didn't need them to change his diapers, he could do that, he didn't want them to remove the sheets and expose him to the lights, Senhor Hélio standing on the fifth step

—I did it

what is it that watches me from the window and is neither people nor trees, it was himself watching just as he used to watch his uncle sitting at his desk, his face in his hands

—I'm not a man

and even a toad wasn't enough to console him, one Saturday his uncle

—I can't bear living in the village

and he was amazed, given how much his uncle liked the trains and the serenity of May, when the clocks stood still

—What time is it?

after what seemed like an eternity him asking again

—What time is it?

his grandmother, as if he hadn't already asked

—Four o'clock

and yet it wasn't that they'd forgotten to wind the clocks, it was time itself forgetting, even time forgets just like his grandfather forgetting to eat, his fork in his mouth, his grandmother

—Come on, then

and perhaps after that last

—You know

his father had forgotten too, he didn't dare ask

—Do I know what, Daddy?

he never did call him

—Daddy

and yet there were times when he did say it quietly to himself

—Daddy

and then feel annoyed by that

—Daddy

remembering that business with the maid

—Please don't tell my wife

and hating him with a vengeance, why the devil are the shelves and the jars rattling, the smile

—I'll help you

and then no jars and no shelves, I have not sinned, Father, I won't come bothering you any more about luxuria, my grandmother running eyes and nose over the page, abundance, sumptuous enjoyment, Old French *luxurie*, Latin *luxuria* from *luxus*, High German *lust*, Gothic *lustus*, Greek λιλαίεσθαι, Sanskrit *las*, the verb to lust, to please, to delight in, to desire excessively, to produce luxuriant growth, the curate shooing him away

—No need to say a single Hail Mary, child, just be quiet

and in his head no luxuria, only

—Leveret

and dead animals dangling from his waist on his way to church, Senhor Hélio

—This time I'm going to make it

clumsily hoicking up his knee, once on the way back from the Mondego an almost naked child

—Bread, bread

and he was amazed at how startled his father was whenever he stumbled over tree roots, my grandmother

—You see, people don't live there

rising up from the undergrowth with weightless ease

—Bread

and my father and me getting more and more nervous as we made our way back to the village, unable to find the right track, my grandmother

—You see, people don't live there

or, rather, more people than I can tell you about live there, the bus empty and the trains empty because the passengers, not that they are passengers, you'll understand one day, get off at the path that leads to the rocks, the stain on the shoe taking his pulse

—His heart rate has increased

and climb with their various bundles up to the lights that we can see from the balcony at night, why else do you think they're keeping you in here if not to protect you from the mountains, it's not because of your illness, it's the looming clouds and the well where the mud talks to us, oh, those wretched chestnut trees, which, if I'd had my way, we would have had cut down, and your grandfather pretending he was deaf because he belonged with those people, he arrived from the mountains bowing and smiling and I didn't have the courage to tell him no just as my parents didn't have the courage to tell him no and so he moved into my life and turned me into one of them, I try to escape without seeming to escape, to move away without seeming to move away, to serve him so discreetly that he forgets all about me, who do you think it was asking

—Bread

but the children he had before he had my children or the grandchildren who were born before you were born, what do you think your father means when he says

—You know

you're not the same blood as me, your blood is the blood of the people on the bus, look at those old ladies wearing shawls

—You'll come with us one day

and I will go with them one day, along with Dona Irene, the curate, all of them, your uncle packing his bag in his bedroom thinking he'd be able to travel to Spain, the fool, no one escapes from the village, we have no blood, we have no flesh, we're withering away, look at my skin, my hands, the dress that's too big for me now because my bones are shrinking, the nurse grabbing him by the legs

—Have you soiled yourself again?

don't believe it, don't deceive yourself, don't get your hopes up, his father and him getting more and more nervous and the church and the cypress trees endlessly rocking, when did the cypresses start rocking, Senhor Hélio having reached the doormat

—Here I am

and the bag of pebbles he carried under his coat jacket slowly becoming his body, what was my heart writing on the screen when he saw me

—You're Antoninho, aren't you?

muddling up the words while I was trying to find my pain, since I'd lost everything else I didn't want to lose my pain, my father

—You know

no, his father saying

—Come on, hurry up

and him not walking down by the rivers, the leaves coming down, the grasshopper's eggs dropping down, a branch from a willow tree spinning down to the ground, no, we weren't walking down by the rivers, Senhor Hélio and my grandfather on the balcony and I couldn't believe that my grandmother had accepted my grandfather out of fear

—Keep peeling the apricots and stop lying

he believed he was going to live and the doctors looked pleased

—Well done, well done

him not in pajamas but wearing the clothes of a healthy man, a little pale, it's true, a little tired, it's true, but healthy, I imagined all that, I invented all that, I got better, I live in a house in Lisbon, in September I'm going back to the village, goodness, how it's changed, factories, traffic circles, a big church, people asking the neighbors

—Do you remember him?

another priest instead of the curate, an esplanade, a lake,

the mountains looking very knowing but friendly, the stain on the shoe to the visitors

—He has moments of lucidity, poor man

what did he mean *moments of lucidity,* the illness has vanished, Senhor Hélio now able to master his words

—You're growing, lad

taller than his father and yet still that

—You know

troubling him, the stain on the shoe

—Moments of lucidity but few and far between

such ignorance, he stuck his leg over the edge of the bed and the nurse tucked it back under the sheets

—Now, now

he tried to explain that he was expected in the village, that the child

—Bread, bread

and that because of the child he had to leave and in his place Senhor Hélio

—You're Antoninho, aren't you?

I'm going to conquer every step, I'm not going to fall face forward onto the tablecloth, no one's going to write a note in shaky capital letters saying that I died and your mother not daring to tear it up, not leaving it on the table, not leaving it in the dresser

—Where shall I put it?

no, his mother now groping the air

—Who are you?

running the tips of her fingers over his face, the stain on the shoe

—You see, he's gone again

and he really had gone again, into a water denser than

water and up above the glittering lights dissolving and re-forming only to dissolve again, he tried to get back on his bike but the pedals were missing, he placed the chestnut on top of the wall so as to crush it with a stone and the cook

—Mind you don't hurt yourself, dear

and at the same time the smile

—That wasn't so hard, was it?

this was in either Lisbon or the village, he couldn't quite remember, what he remembered was the doctor saying

—We're going to have to operate

and him shrinking back in fear, the whole strange world around him and in his mind

—It might be perfectly easy

he asked his dead father

—That wasn't so hard, was it?

thinking they had mistaken his results for someone else's, they belong to some other man, not me, I'm Antoni-nho, I have two false teeth, I learned to ride a bike when I was seven, I experience moments of real contentment when my father

—You know

perhaps wanting to warn him, at the source of the Mondego tiny frogs sitting on pebbles, the doctor waiting and he was surprised that his life should depend on such a very ordinary guy saying

—Just a moment

in order to answer the phone

—I'll ring you later, but in principle yes

and him realizing that he was no longer part of life, the doctor's fingers wandering over the desk, creating objects that weren't there before he touched them, and him

—Look, a stapler

an owl with a stethoscope

—Where did that owl come from?

a ring-binder diary open at the wrong date and him wanting to put that right, why do diaries insist on what once was,
he had a diary too but he never leafed through it, why would
he, don't say

—You know

Dad, be quiet, it's not that I'm not grateful for your help,
it's just that you can't do anything for me, the doctor picked
up a pen, then put it down again

—Would you like a week to think it over?

think what over, how, go back home inside a body he
knew but that no longer belonged to him, he looked down
at his hands and said

—Hands

but whose hands was he talking to, the doctor's, his, he
remembered the encouraging smile and turned his face to
that smile, what a strange month March was, such a hesitant
spring, Virgílio's cart waiting on a corner, his uncle helping
Senhor Hélio down the steps and his mother

—Anyone would think you were a young man

dear God, a whole week, seven pages in the ring-binder
diary that he would leave blank and his heart writing an endless lament, he said

—Don't interrupt me

when no one was interrupting him, no one was knocking at his door, no one came looking for him apart from the
child from the mountains

—Bread, bread

he could hear the echo of a quarry where the stone breakers were hammering away and Dona Irene brought her harp, massaging her fingers

—It's been years since I played

on the surface of the water denser than water the glittering lights, he has occasional lucid moments but these are becoming few and far between, the stain on the shoe

—Generally speaking, these patients

and he stopped listening, he was listening to the abyss of the ward and the curate

—Leveret

his uncle walking past him

—Antoninho

the bishop was blessing the rockroses and not a parishioner in sight, the curate's housekeeper offering him a bunch of grapes

—So you'll remember us when you go away

and boots waiting at the front door ready to start walking, he suddenly remembered seeing a snake in the garden, he picked up a brick to kill it but the snake escaped, the first note from the harp came down to meet him mingled with the pain that wasn't exactly pain

—I promise you won't feel any pain

and he didn't care about the pain, he cared about his seventeen-year-old smile

—Come on, then

and him fearfully buttoning up his coat

—I can't, I don't know how

beyond the balcony a building with a limp flag attached to the top of the pole, windows from which they spied on him and doubtless knew who he was

—It's Antoninho, isn't it?

the doctor

—Senhor Antunes

and he was surprised at that

—Senhor Antunes

because you don't address a seventeen-year-old lad as Senhor Antunes, you say

—Boy

or

—Child

his body grows plump with a sigh

—Oh, to be your age again

and then they so completely forget us that they don't even notice we're removing the IV drip, the diaper, the catheter, picking up our clothes and racing to the train station where several months' worth of newspapers are waiting in piles for my grandfather to read, except that he won't read them, we walk around the foot of the mountains, the wasps pursue us for a while, then give up, and even though our father standing next to the source of the Mondego says

—You know

and a child says

—Bread, bread

we don't sit down with them, we spread our arms wide like the red kites and turn and drift endlessly, weightlessly, on the air.

29 March 2007

Now that he no longer wanted anything and everything was a matter of indifference to him, there was no village and no Lisbon, there was only a fly perched somewhere between his face and his hand rubbing its slender legs together, and he needed nothing at all apart from that fly, a companion, a colleague, he was afraid the fly might leave him, he felt like asking it

—Stay with me

because he wasn't interested in his visitors, just as he wasn't interested in what had been or what the future might hold, years in a provincial house collapsing stone by stone behind the ivy, the fly on one of his eyelids now and the fly's presence consoled him as something that might at least stay with him

—He seems to sleep more and more

and he wasn't sleeping, he was watching time, even though time didn't move and his organs didn't move, his brain was probably still working, though, because he could see himself running along beneath the April rain heading somewhere or other or writing to God at Christmas and God replying, although when it came to the electric train set, God delegated his words to his grandmother

—God thinks it's very expensive

and he was amazed that God should know about prices and keep accounts like her in a school notebook with, on the cover, a little girl in braids playing with a hoop and, on the back, the multiplication table, the fly exchanged his eyelid for the washbasin, still energetically rubbing its legs together, and the little girl all night

—Bread, bread

underneath the balcony, stopping them from sleeping with her monotonous prayer until his grandmother finally handed her a piece of bread, which the girl continued to gaze at without accepting, she would hide among the fig trees and return at dusk, she wasn't just underneath the balcony, she was in the chicken run, in the shed, in what had once been the winery, and beyond her were vestiges of other people, not the old ladies in their shawls but silhouettes moving noiselessly about in the bushes, his grandmother pointing to one of them

—My godfather

drinking water from the bucket at the well

—You never really took any notice of me, Ofélia

with the scar from a knife fight on his face and one eyetooth protruding from under his lip

—I am an eyetooth

while bits of storks' nests dribbled down the chimney, when his grandfather died he was touched to see the objects he had kept on his bedside table, especially the rabbit's foot, meant to bring luck to the bedroom, the mirror not knowing what to do

—Now what am I supposed to reflect?

and it was reflecting him, now fat now thin, depending on the quality of the glass, him examining himself

—Good afternoon, Antoninho

the rabbit's foot on the key ring, him imagining what it might open and afraid of turning the key in the lock, his grandfather would probably be there behind the lock

—Haven't you noticed, I'm not here anymore?

hiding a slipper under the chest of drawers, removing a note, remembering he was dead and leaving it on the top while he was thinking about the money of the dead, how they earn it and who accepts their loose change, his father and his uncle wore his clothes but neither of them read the newspaper on the balcony, Senhor Hélio was just about to reach the first step, then he remembered the funeral and went back down in a complicated maneuver, knocking over a flowerpot and walking off beneath the orphaned chestnut trees to find himself in the square, shuffling his fingers in a game of solitaire for phalanges, asking him

—Would you like me to talk to you?

but he had already placed his fingers on a board and was beginning to turn them over to see the card, how the world changes when we look closely, everything grows larger, murmurs, transforms, it wasn't the nurses looking after him, it was the murmurings in his grandfather's bedroom, one day he plucked up the courage to enter the vet's abandoned house and found a lady sitting on a rocking chair making lace

—I'm his daughter-in-law

he took his uncle, they skirted round a dried-up pond where there was an even more dried-up sparrow surrounded by ants, they chose the back door with one glass pane missing, went down a corridor, a living room, an invalid's crutches, went up to the first floor by some stairs intent on escaping from them both

—You're stepping on me

his uncle aware of the suffering of things

—Sorry

with which he enjoyed an enviable intimacy, and a sky-light full of startled bats, a wooden horse perhaps belonging to the little girl demanding

—Bread, bread

cat poo but no cat, no one has ever actually seen a cat, we think they belong to us but in reality we invent them just as I invented this illness, which in turn invents me and invents the hospital, the doctors and the fantasy of dying, my grandfather didn't die, he's in his room slipping the rabbit's foot into the locks of the air, he turns it and the office where he worked in the city with his colleagues appears, his colleagues greeting him

—We thought you'd retired

he turns it again and his father is holding up a broken jug

—Did you break this?

my grandfather's father a postcard in a drawer, back Thursday miss you, which my grandfather studied angrily, why did *back Thursday miss you* upset my grandfather so much, the stain on the shoe while he was thinking about the thousand languages of the waves

—He's slowly fading, but don't worry, he's not in any pain

and he wasn't in any pain as he pondered that postcard, there it was and the ink hadn't aged at all, miss you, which meant he was alive somewhere, about to arrive from who knows where, on Thursdays he went down to the train station, where his grandfather's father didn't get off the train, only the newspapers did, thrown from the carriage by a pair of invisible arms, and it intrigued him that the newspapers continued to shift about on the ground like entrails, the pharmacist got off the train wearing a new suit and saying to the guard telling the trains to depart with a wave of his flag

—What a woman

in a moment of sated glory, and a girl struggling with a live duck under one arm, possibly his grandfather's mother there before him on the platform until long after the smoke had vanished and then the fir trees again, her and a dog that didn't belong to her on the deserted platform, dogs, unlike cats, do exist, they keep close to us, don't let us go, why invent cats if they always despise us, they disappear behind their eyelids and then their eyelids disappear into the folds of their bodies, of course we invented them, they never existed, they don't exist, Dona Irene convinced that she lived with a cat

—My cat

so as to avoid the terrifying thought that she was living alone, leaving a saucer of milk and a small litter box on the floor, she would keep watch in the morning on the saucer full of milk and the untouched litter box, believing so firmly in the cat's existence that she would sometimes see a little nose appear around her armchair and call

—Pussycat

but there was only the armchair, believe me, cats don't exist, I'm not lying, back Thursday miss you and so my grandfather's mother was waiting in her old-fashioned dress and in the certainty that people do come back, today, tomorrow, next week, or perhaps that was just a hope as well, his uncle intrigued by the wooden horse

—Tell me that story about the daughter-in-law again

who may have believed in cats too and his uncle murmuring the way people do in dreams

—I knew the vet

he knew the vet and knew the daughter-in-law, always
completely enclosed in deepest mourning, to whom the curate with God inside a cup would go and give Communion
at the house, the hospital chaplain didn't give Communion
at all, he merely pressed his thumb down on his forehead,
making the sign of the cross

—Such a shame

and consulted with the stain on the shoe about his knee
that had to be hoisted up when he got to his feet during the
Eucharist

—What could the problem be, Doctor?

the stain on the shoe, checking the IV drip, suggesting
a massage might help, the fly tempted the chaplain, who
caught it in his hand, turned on the faucet over the washbasin, put the fly under the tap and flushed it down the drain

—Filthy thing

which made him doubt the catechism, his uncle stood utterly still in the vet's house, like a gundog ready to race off

—Can't you feel the presence of people here?

and he couldn't feel the presence of people there, he
could hear the hawthorns in the garden rubbing against one
another, he felt afraid, he felt hungry, he thought he saw a
unicorn appear behind a low table and was startled at the
sight, he wished his mother was by his side, he wished his
father

—You know

not daring to touch him and just as well he didn't, when

he returned the tennis ball he held it with the tips of his fingers so that his father's hand would not touch his and yet today, if his father were still alive, he would like to say

—Touch me

even if they weren't standing by the source of the Mondego, the part where the mountains are scorched brown, and in the part where the mountains hadn't burned, gorse bushes telling our story ever since we were born, my father

—You know

and please don't touch Senhor Antunes, touch me, call me *son,* even before he died when he still called people by their name, he didn't say

—Son

his father

—You

and inside that

—You

perhaps a discreet

—Son

if only I could go with him to the Englishmen's hotel, to the pine forest, to the orchard with my head just level with his chest, if his father reached out an arm to help him up a hill he would pretend he was fine and avoid him, his uncle insisting

—Can't you feel the presence of people here?

and of course he could, not just the lady in the rocking chair but other presences too, the pharmacist in his new suit saying to the guard signaling to the trains to leave

—What a woman

strangers who died before he was born talking about the wolves near the school during the grubby whiteness of winter, at night even the most far distant of sounds became close neighbors and the earth's axis, in need of oil, imposed itself on the clocks, canceling out time, why didn't you send a postcard, Uncle, arrive Thursday miss you, I thought I could see him approaching from my pillow

—I've got your bicycle downstairs

it had a wheel missing, the light wasn't working, but it was otherwise all right, thank heavens, him pedaling and his uncle with his hand on the saddle until he got left behind and was lost, don't go to the well, Uncle, don't go to Spain, at what point on the Mondego do the fish start, at what point in the fish do the seagulls start, at what point in the seagulls will the boats start, boats that are reflected not in the water but in the air, what did the people in the vet's house who were listening to the seagulls want when they wondered

—Does the lad remind you of someone?

the March rain on the window and his organs continuing to write in their coded language, similar to that of the grown-ups round the table, whom he understood only when they told him off about his manners

—Don't stick your chin in the bowl

his father not correcting anything

—Can't you teach your son to behave?

and he didn't teach his son to behave, he always seemed to be thinking about something else, although quite what he didn't know, he tended the orchard and made apples by forming a round shape with his hands, then he would hold them up and when he parted them there was a fruit, he would stick one finger into the soil and bring out a cricket, such a shame there were no apples or crickets in the hospital, an empty void of waiting and at three o'clock in the afternoon other people's relatives, intimidated by the silence hemming in all the sounds and the slowly pulsating pains belonging to someone or other

—You know

the last time he came to see him he formed that same round shape with his hands but instead of creating an apple or producing a cricket, when he parted his hands they were empty

—I can't do it anymore

and him wondering if he had lost a tennis ball in the bushes, even today, when he didn't care about anything, he was wondering if he'd lost a tennis ball in the bushes, trying to remember every single bush, every hole, every clump of grass, and he would discover grasshoppers, beetles, slugs, what he thought was a toad and wasn't a toad, a stone or else a toad with no legs, he and the stone looking at each other, he touched it with the tip of his shoe and nothing happened, if he hadn't been in the hospital he would have stuffed it in his pocket so as to study it later in stunned amazement, his mother

—Are you collecting stones, dear?

and he collected stones just as he collected the dry corpses of horseflies, bent nails, cocoons, the marvels out of which he was creating the world, it wasn't his father that worried him, it was the absence of the tennis ball, the suspicion that his father

—Son

and the importance of that

—Son

and what to do with it, bring the rocking chair from the vet's house and dance around it swearing

—I am your father

however many times you want, I don't mind, even in the hospital I could hear

—Son

the stain on the shoe

—Now and then his heart rate becomes erratic

No, not his heart, disparate words in a scrap of memory

—What a woman

the barber tilting his cheek with his warm hands and him watching his cut hair falling onto the towel

—You've got a whole sackful of wool there

and now just a few fine hairs on his yellow skin, the barber

—What happened to the wool?

indignant that he could have been so careless as he picked up his tools, limping along in his white jacket, as a boy he used to walk past the barber's shop imitating that limp while the barber, he couldn't remember his name, was snipping neatly away at Senhor Hélio's moustache, his moustache all sorts of colors, starting off brown and becoming paler near his nose, the barber disguising the brown

—If I hadn't stopped smoking I'd be puffing out steam now like a pot on the stove

by applying a little white dye with a brush, then he would notice me and limp clumsily over to get his razor

—I'll slit your throat, you little rascal

and he would run home, not even noticing Dona Lucrécia

—Come here, boy

once the cortege of turtledoves had carried them all off he would limp alone through the village, among the pigeons in the square and not beneath the March rain in the hospital, the smells of August that he missed so much, the nurse to the colleague helping him change the catheter bag

—What did he do before he was in here?

and if he could have answered he would have said

—I waited for my grandfather's father at the station

arrive Thursday miss you, but he never did arrive, the surprise and the horror had disappeared days ago and in the intervals between sleep he searched for the person he had once been, and in the morning a strange discovery

—I'm me

these pajamas, this face, he was imagining that he had no body and suddenly that discovery, and it was full of discomforts, tiredness, the shock of being given a name and being spoken to, his grandmother

—Would you like to taste the jam?

before filling the jars, picking things up without even looking at them or else the things obediently came to her, he didn't mind them changing his diaper nor that his private parts were on view, they were washing someone else, not him, he was merely present, the nurse from behind the pain

—There you are, you rascal, clean as a whistle

just like his mother behind her apron drying him after his bath in the tub, the pump for the well right next to the kitchen, it's forty years since his mother dried him

—Will it be much longer, Doctor?

the workers from the tungsten mine outside the church, hats pulled well down, they didn't seem to be suffering, why is it that ever since he fell ill the village refuses to leave him, there's the maid collecting eggs from the chicken run, shooing away the hens, she would place the eggs in his hand still warm, there's the frost in February and the idle snow full of echoes, it wasn't Lisbon that came to him, it was the village, two or three big houses and some poor people's shacks, and what binds me to this and what makes me return without realizing something I thought I had forgotten, my grandmother's dressing gown hanging from a nail, a drunk finding his hands in his pockets, removing them and continuing on his way with his sleeves empty, the nurse

—He's not thinking about anything

and he wasn't thinking about anything, he could see the rain on the window and his grandmother complaining about October because the water whistled in her bones, he could see the Englishmen's hotel where the roof was beginning to give way, and the lawn around the swimming pool had been replaced by weeds, although the blonde foreigner was still there picking up her towel, he couldn't see the hospital or the stain on the shoe

—To be perfectly honest, it's not an easy situation

so simple to say for someone outside the difficult situation but he didn't notice the man, he noticed the ribbon round his wrist, and what could he be hoping for from that ribbon, the stain on the shoe trying to cheer him up

—We have more resources nowadays

the ribbon almost wearing thin, the doctor probably hoping it would protect him from a chestnut like his, one of the hotel's chimneys crumbled and fell into the flower bed and the crows cawed cruelly, in the autumn they lumbered from tree to tree, the cook put out any leftovers for them and the crows and the dogs

—We have more resources nowadays

fought over them in a flurry of feathers

—To be perfectly honest, it's not an easy situation

and he smiled at the thought that the barber wouldn't have to paint his moustache, nor would he be found playing solitaire with his fingers, Senhor Hélio used to manage the Cooperative and yet if you mentioned this to him he would pause for a moment, incredulous

—The Cooperative?

the word *Cooperative* was familiar to him but he didn't know why, an office, barrels, buffalo with withered dewlaps, everything so vague, so pale, a woman who addressed him as

—Dad

and him entirely focused on his fingers, the woman who addressed him as

—Dad

was saying to a creature wearing glasses

—We'll have to think about putting him in a home

in a place where shapeless creatures sat dozing in orthopedic chairs, Dona Lurdes, Dona Amália, the engineer Oliveira, he was beginning to feel irritated by the ribbon worn by the stain on the shoe, would it or wouldn't it break, a hand on his shoulder

—It'll all be fine, Senhor Antunes

and of course it will all be fine, my friend, even if the dogs carry me off piece by piece, everything's already fine, don't you see, my heart and my liver hesitate but then begin again, the pain comes sniffing around if I get distracted but it doesn't bother me, it stops, it's January, my friend, not March, the lamps lit at four in the afternoon and surrounding the lamps the night, the stain on the shoe restoring his shoulder to him

—Contrary to what you might think, I'm not disappointed

well, thank God neither of us is disappointed, my friend, it isn't October as it is in the village and the water isn't whistling in my grandmother's bones and the ivy hasn't started to lose its tendrils, the wolves are leaving the school and I'm in the hospital unaware of my empty body, as you said looking away and not at me

—We have more resources nowadays

and we have the bus and the well, people lean over the edge and not a glimmer from the mud beneath, first the outline of a stone and then darkness, my uncle

—Can you still do figure eights?

and not a single granite pillar to prevent me from leaving.

30 March 2007

At night they turned off all the lights in his room apart from the small bare bulb that his grandmother left on to protect him from the dark, the ivy branches tapping on the window calling to him, although the name they called wasn't his but that of someone who had occupied the room before him or who would take up residence afterward when they took him away, often when he went out and again turned the key in the lock, he would stand on the doormat and look back at the house without him inside it and everything seemed different, the furniture, the color of the walls, even the shape of the living room waiting for some new arrival, who was perhaps already in the kitchen or in the bedroom, in fact it seemed to him that he could hear footsteps and drawers being opened and closed, all this on the very edge of silence yet very much present, alive, he would hesitate to go in, afraid they might throw him out, and so he remained there on the doormat, polite, embarrassed, one of the visitors

—He looks better today

No, he didn't, at any moment those footsteps would approach at a pace very similar to his and a stranger would be standing, equally motionless, staring at him and wearing a jacket no longer his, clothes that had once been his, features he had ceased to have, and he would close the door, going down the stairs, pulling off a leaf from the plant in the hallway as he usually did, peering up at the balcony from the pavement opposite, the keys in his pocket suddenly feeling so like alien presences that he would throw them guiltily into one of the trash cans, certain he was being watched from above because two fingers opened the curtain just a smidgeon and whose were those fingers, where could he go at night once he'd walked past the building and seen some guy fixing the pelmet and a woman on the balcony, and yet he lived alone, the remaining buildings all looked different too, the bank branch where the clerk who usually served him didn't even say hello, his regular table on the café terrace was occupied by someone else, and the little boy with the toy plane who always smiled at him completely ignored him, what was the name on his ID and what were these objects in his pocket, the visitors saying

—He looks better today

who were they referring to, he turned back and groped around in the trash can but couldn't find the keys, he found only things belonging to a stranger, he tried to remember the mountains but there were no mountains in his head, no village, no river, no sobbing harp, no Senhor Casimiro reaching into the candy jar up to his elbow

—Have you been a good boy?

he imagined Virgílio's cart rattling along the bramble-lined path but it wasn't, it was a municipal van and some workmen, one of them wearing glasses, repairing a fire hydrant, I must be in Lisbon but which part, for God's sake, the lights he went through jerkily changing colors, the woman hanging out a child's pajamas taking pegs out of a little basket she didn't have, so where does the child sleep, in the attic, where even the smallest cradle would be in the way, in the storeroom, in a corner of the living room

—He looks better today

how dare they say he looked better when they didn't even know who he was, the stain on the shoe

—Senhor Antunes

calling him by the wrong name, there was no more Senhor Antunes, what's my surname, why am I here, he didn't feel ill, he was a bit annoyed that they'd turned out the lights, someone else's memories diverting him from the past and no trains and no bishop, they tied him to the bed with strips of sheet

—He's starting to drift off

and as he drifted whole flocks of images came to him, a boy in a recliner coughing into a bottle, a man with a sack over his shoulder getting off a steamship and picking him up

—Is this my nephew, Luísa?

alien existences invading his, episodes he had no idea how to deal with, the memory of the porch came to him only to be lost, the boy in the recliner thanking him for his visit

—It's lucky you came

him saying nothing

—It's lucky I came?

and the boy looking out over a landscape of holm oaks whose perfume soothed them both, how good oak trees smell in May, the certainty that it was May and that the earth was growing, when he turned round a lady was there arranging flowers

—You never wrote to me again, Alfredo

breathing whispered complaints into his ear, if only the

blonde foreigner at the Englishmen's hotel breathed like that, the lady's complaints growing louder

—You were very cruel to me

and the stain on the shoe studying the results of various tests and drawing circles round certain numbers

—Slow the rate of the IV drip

he whispered to the lady

—Who's living in my house?

dark waves breaking against the seawall, oily patches, bits of straw, the doctor who was neither Senhor Antunes nor Alfredo preoccupied with the drip

—Twenty drops a minute maximum

which he hardly heard because the guy adjusting the drip was hurting him, he tried to talk to the woman and show her his new keys

—Who had these made for me?

so that she could explain each key one by one, the key for the downstairs door and the upstairs door, the key to the beach house, because there was sure to be a beach house where the tide didn't reach, the sound of the waves wouldn't let him sleep, her mouth like a slimy snail trail on his chest

—You won't run away again, will you?

handcuffing him with a yearning sweetness that made an unexpected belly spring to life inside his belly, the lady's brooch sticking in him, a hairpin sticking in him, her ring sticking in him, the nurse to the stain on the shoe

—I can't find a vein

and the ring

—You won't run away again, will you?

out in the hospital corridor he heard the rattle of plates on the little aluminum lunch cart with one wheel slower than the others, where was he and where could he escape to, he just couldn't get used to the past he'd been given and so he tried to bring the village closer to him, he managed to retrieve a church, but it wasn't the same church, it had no cemetery next to it nor any of the sick people from the tungsten mine in the square outside, he looked for signs of the wolves, and the church and the sick people from the tungsten mine whirled up into the air and were lost, if he wanted to see his street he couldn't find it in Lisbon, instead he found the little park and the Pakistani store where he used to do his shopping, but everything else was absent, the insurance agency next to the travel agent's, whose employees stood out on the pavement smoking, the faces of the bus passengers painted on the windows like the faces of the firemen in the toy metal fire engine he was given as a boy, complete with emergency escape ladder, now and then some of those faces evaporated from the windows and got off at a stop transformed into people, he was surprised they had torsos, arms, legs and could walk, a first, hesitant step and then, once they'd got used to it, heading off round a corner, the car showroom had vanished too and there were dozens of small side gates he had never noticed before, the guy who disembarked from the steamship put him down on the ground

—Goodness, they grow up fast, Luísa

and the person he was calling Luísa was invisible, and there was possibly a man accompanying her, because beside her was a void filled only by a match and a lit cigarette, the stain on the shoe was checking the rate of the IV drip on his watch

—Yes, leave it like that

as if he were in the hospital, which, of course, he wasn't,

he could hear wild trees and the gargling of waves, the lady arranging the flowers

—Thank you

thanking him for what, he tried to hear the one o'clock fast train and the travelers who hid instead of getting off, he felt sorry for her, having to live in the house, because the bucket under the cracked pipe in the bathroom kept dripping despite the sacking he'd wrapped around it, he said

—Mom

without meaning to because he wasn't even thinking about her, he was thinking about the red kites waiting for a hen to leave the chicken run in order to dive down and alarm the dogs, he didn't mention the cats, because, as he had proved, they were insubstantial beings, small mica pebbles that people mistook for eyes leading around a shadow that materialized on walls, away from the walls they were at most a delicate little finger on the piano keys of the floorboards or a shiver on the roof tiles, but the roof tiles might be owls that had lost their way, his father raised his nose for a second, then carried on eating, barely touching his knife and fork, which moved of their own accord and resisted any interference, his mother

—Where are your manners?

and it wasn't his fault, it was the objects making fun of him, for example, when he picked up his glass he had to say

—I'm going to pick up my glass

and he gripped it hard so as not to drop it, the surprise and terror reaching out as far as his chest

—I'm going to die

and they left him because he wasn't Senhor Antunes in a Lisbon hospital, and because he wasn't Senhor Antunes he remained eternal, with dozens of weeks ahead of him, months, years, the boy in the recliner

—Don't you think I look better?

not demanding the truth, begging for lies so that he could lie to himself, how strange they look, those empty shoes with empty socks inside, who's hiding away in the clothes on the hangers, squeeze them and there's no one there, don't squeeze them and there they are, people hanging alongside one another, if he were to go home, which he wouldn't, the shelves would draw back in astonishment

—You?

and him incapable of orienting himself in the altered rooms, a divan where the dresser stood, the tablecloth with a mark that used to be covered by a jug and his telephone ringing for intruders, the lady with the flowers

—You never wrote me again, Alfredo

he who never wrote to anyone, they don't answer our letters, in the mail he would find brochures that he would then put in his neighbors' mailboxes and which then returned to his, if someone sent him a postcard, arrive Thursday miss you, he didn't believe it and even if a passenger got off the one o'clock fast train he wouldn't go over to him, the lady with the flowers

—Come with me, Alfredo

and the one o'clock fast train drowned in pine trees, his father

—Now I can tell you

and just when his father was about to speak he woke up with the nurse giving him a pill

—Swallow it, Senhor Antunes

after the pill, back to the pillow again exhausted, and the lady with the flowers ironing his trousers

—You don't take enough care of yourself

pleased to be looking after him, you could tell by her gestures, she would scrape off any stubborn stains and then carry on with her ironing, the man off the steamship

—You took advantage of my absence to become a man

and him feeling guilty for having become a man in the midst of all the sacks and bundles, then from the harbor to the city, not the road leading to the Englishmen's hotel or the road into the mountains, avenues and squares growing ever less distinct as he fell asleep, his grandmother lost forever

—Antoninho

realizing her mistake and saying

—Alfredo

shacks on a hillside, a viaduct, a road, his father was talking to him and sleep prevented him from hearing, he replied, conscious that not a syllable

—Speak more loudly, Dad

as he plunged into a torpor peopled by faded shapes, the doctor

—It's only natural he should come and go like this

the organs on the screen vague smudges, his eyes could make out the lady with the flowers

—Not much longer, wait

and since that didn't depend on him he couldn't wait, just as the boots didn't wait for him, they set off toward the pine forest or the church, he wasn't quite sure, the boy in the recliner invited him to take his pulse

—What do you think?

the weak six o'clock sun in the village and a chaffinch setting the top of a tree trembling, Virgílio's cousin used to fry them on the front steps, fat dripping onto a slice of bread and him spitting the little bones into an empty can, he realized that his father was giving him an explanation, but the explanation didn't satisfy him, the fact is there's no explanation for anything, the boy all fingers drawing the blanket up to his chin, hoping for a protection that didn't appear, the wind forcing open the doors in search of the place it had come from, I don't want this past, I want the chestnut trees, the ash trees, my uncle instead of the man from the steamship, the one who will never come back from Spain, drain the well and there are teeth beneath the water, he could feel his own teeth emerge from behind the miniature curtains of his lips and they'll take my place, the only things that weren't given their own personal screen on which they could write their story, the lady with the flowers put away the ironing board and the iron and hung her apron up among the dish towels

—One moment, Alfredo

he imagined her smoothing her hair or opening the little box containing her earrings and hesitating between two pairs, trying on each pair, this one, then that, to study the effect, suburban buildings, a school, in his school the teacher saying not

—Antoninho

but quick as a flash

—Antunes

and then

—Antunes, list the tributaries of the Tejo

not the one you follow down to the estuary, to the right of

the school a creature with a walking stick who looked rather like the man getting off the steamship

—I thought you weren't coming, Luísa

while he was wondering what Luísa would be like, he knew her skirt and her blouse but her neck was too far away for him to reach her face, despite his being tied to the bed they threw him out of the car and didn't even offer him a stretcher but hauled him onto his feet

—He's almost dropping with fatigue

and how could he explain that it wasn't fatigue, it was the chestnut growing, the stain on the shoe

—He won't walk again

and in the end he did, surprise installed itself in him like the tide drawing back leaving behind tiny acid pebbles and a lament from the seaweed before the seagulls ate it, the eleven o'clock freight train passed the balcony with all its cars closed, sometimes at the station he caught a glimpse of a young calf through a missing plank and recoiled, the lady with the flowers holding an earring

—Can you close this clasp?

and without his reading glasses he couldn't, the lady turned on the lamp and turned her ear to the light, he saw the eye of a calf through the missing plank and recoiled, the stationmaster

—You'll be eating him next week, boy

and for months afterward as soon as supper was served he would explore his plate with his fork, his grandmother

—What's wrong with you, child?

and how could he convince his grandmother that it was wrong to eat a friend, the clasp on the earring almost slipped from his fingers but he managed to hold on to it, if he found an eye on his plate he would faint for sure, the doctor studying the screen

—He's had a very slight spasm

of course he'd had a very slight spasm, what a surprise, a very slight spasm, he almost shot him a sardonic glance, his teacher

—Not a single river?

while his fat classmate could name fourteen, he wanted to be a chimney sweep or a minister and he was neither a chimney sweep nor a minister, he had inherited his father's haberdashery shop and apart from the source of the Mondego he had never visited any rivers and eventually the names of rivers emptied of meaning, words that he had kept all his life just as people keep empty medicine bottles, why so many rivers, and measuring lengths of cotton velvet with a wooden tape measure and stealing a few inches along the way, the lady with the flowers turned out the light, having first made sure her earrings were securely fastened

—You're not very good with your hands, are you?

and the calf's eye would not leave his thoughts in the midst of all those backs and tails, straw chewed slowly with no sense of time, they swallowed it, then summoned it back up to be swallowed all over again, fourteen rivers, honestly, who could remember fourteen rivers nowadays, the creature with the walking stick

—What I wouldn't give to have my family with me today

a little room smaller than his with a shelf full of miniature animals given away in cereal packets, a crocodile with huge jaws, hippos, elephants, and a concertina on a hook, they made him drink a drop of liqueur that tasted of insomnia and the doctor said in alarm

—Another slight spasm, gentlemen

at the same time as the creature with the walking stick

—Your son doesn't seem to like the taste, Luísa

the photograph of the boy in the recliner declaring

—The worst is over

his face creased up with coughing, he suspected that some of the cars on the freight train were full of boys on recliners announcing

—The worst is over

and so when he went back to the village he would peer through the cracks in the planks of the railcars convinced he could hear a cry for help, he asked the man with the flag

—Where are they taking them, Senhor Liberto?

and Senhor Liberto said nothing, one day they'll unplug all the screens and he'll be in a railcar too, aware of the pine forests going by and the little girl

—Bread, bread

his visitors scouring the cars looking for him

—Antoninho

on the village station platform, he imagined that at night, when only the one bulb left on by his grandmother could soothe him, the ivy pronouncing a name that was not his, neither

—Antoninho

nor

—Alfredo

perhaps the name of the man who actually lived in the house, leaving him a stranger outside on the doormat, he imagined that at night the sick people from the tungsten mines were piled into the railcars because that would mean fewer berets growing wrinkled in the sun, even though the mine was closed there was still a phosphorescent glow from the tunnels and a lost miner now near, now far carrying his lunch pack in his hand, they would open the doors of the railcar in the abattoir, call them not by their names, which they didn't have, what names could the poor have, poking them with a stick

—Move along

and the berets falling off one by one but no protests, no one protests in the village, we say yes, what do you gain by disobeying the person in charge, at supper he would shout

—Don't bring me my plate

whenever a train down below hid itself in the pantry and reappeared bit by bit, nose, knee, and finally the whole thing, and the lady with the flowers

—Where were you, Alfredo?

the dinner cart in the hospital corridor frightened him with its wobbly wheel and then the clashing aluminum trays, people complaining

—Why did they choose me?

and why get angry, they chose you and that's that, it happens to everyone, you'll be free soon enough to walk along with the other dead, looking for what you no longer have, and what's the point of looking if you can't find it, the things that belonged to you have vanished or are crumbling away in the cellar, the lady with the flowers handing him his trousers

—At least you'll look smart, Alfredo

no perfume, no makeup, dressed all in black, give me back what's mine, give me a month or two because a month is eternal, I'll say

—Thank you

to the lady with the flowers like my mother in Senhor Casimiro's store

—Say *thank you*

and Senhor Casimiro excusing him

—He's just a lad

fancy calling him a lad, ever since he can remember he's considered himself an adult, if he wanted he could read the newspaper, play tennis at the Englishmen's hotel, marry the blonde foreigner, and he regretted not having married, he showed his grandmother the wedding ring bought at the fair

—I got married

his grandmother studying the ring

—It's not gold, it's tin

and what difference did that make, he showed it to the cook and the cook said very respectfully

—Yes indeed

while she tied his napkin around his neck

—Well, now that you're married don't drop your food

was it his fault if the rice kept falling off his spoon, the blonde foreigner wore no wedding ring and yet she was obviously married, the eucalyptuses knew, the ash trees knew and the fact that the eucalyptuses and the ash trees knew was enough for him, he informed Virgílio

—I'm not a child, I'm a gentleman

and Virgílio giving him a look he preferred not to decipher

—A gentleman

not letting him take the reins or sit on the driver's seat with him

—Get in the back with the potatoes, otherwise this old jalopy might overturn he consoled himself by thinking that the bishop always sat in the back seat and a deacon of no importance sat in the front seat, the bishop would offer his gloved hand to be kissed in between blessings while the old ladies in black

—Excellency

and the bells pealing out in festive mood, they poured more liquor into him among the hippos and the crocodiles

—Another little drop, it isn't every day the family gets together

and a dizziness, a weight, the man from the steamship praising him

—He can hold his liquor like an admiral

the little room swaying to right and left, imitating the tides, the man from the steamship

—I can tell we share the same blood, he can hold his drink as well as me

and he was holding his liquor while hunched up on the sofa, where an awkward spring was sticking in his back, the nurse

—Nothing in his diaper

doubtless strong blood, the woman called Luísa putting her arm around his shoulders

—I think he's fallen asleep, poor thing

and that was a lie, he could see the backs of the buildings, winter mud, a courtyard, he thought *I belong to this place or to this village,* to his mother's delight he said

—Thank you

to Senhor Casimiro and to his wife who was always so easily moved

—What a sweet thank-you

his mother proud of that sweet thank-you

—He's a little love when he wants to be

not realizing that love was in a railcar full of cattle peering through the cracks, not realizing that one of his eyes

—Mom

when Senhor Liberto waved the flag and the train set off, the stain on the shoe

—Have a look at my heart

the platform shrank and nothing but trees, the outskirts of the village lost, the lady with the flowers

—Alfredo

and him observing her closely, incapable of responding.

31 March 2007

Or still more pasts, his life was full of pasts and he didn't know which was the real one, layers of memories superimposed one on top of the other, contradictory recollections, images he didn't know and couldn't imagine belonging to him, and then, without warning, he started getting pains in his spine and in his shoulder and he was nothing but spine and shoulder, the rest didn't count, his ears listening not to the sounds outside but to the pain's conversation, in which a voice kept repeating the same phrase but without decoding its meaning for him, perhaps it belonged to one of the visitors or to those various pasts they had given him in the hospital to distract him from the illness

—Here you are

so many fantasies in his head, a gentleman playing the piano, a scream while he was sleeping and him thinking

—Was that me?

the little dog standing tremulously on its back legs as it licked his fingers just as he would lick any fingers that stroked his face, the gentleman playing the piano turned to look at him and nodded, if at least he could summon up a single tear out of the darkness that was him, around the village he found stones that cry, they didn't ooze geckos or wasps as granite usually did, just a little comma of water, really

—It can't be

you run a finger over it and it's wet, his grandmother

—A tear?

she runs her finger over it and it's dry, with his uncle, though, you knew he was crying not because of the sound he made, there was no sound apart from the pine trees and the crockery, which would now and then announce

—I'm a tureen, I'm a plate

afraid that people might forget, objects are so fragile

—I'm for drinking out of, I'm for storing stuff away in

including the wind that served to blow the gate shut, the pain moved from his shoulder to his arm and the man playing the piano turned round

—How are you?

his grandmother listening to the godfather who appeared to her in the mirrors

—Am I in the way?

and only she noticed

—Godfather Apolinário sends greetings

a shadow in a hat enduring the bus journey from the city despite his bad back, if you peered in through the windows you would see only shabby seats and a hen with its legs bound and its beak tied shut and its throat swelling with fear, perhaps a present that his Godfather Apolinário had forgotten or the driver's lunch to be plucked when he parked up along the road, one afternoon his Godfather Apolinário's wife arrived with her husband saying urgently to my grandmother

—Did you lose the ring I gave you?

having searched for weeks in vases and boxes and among the sheets

—What ring?

even in the suspiciously empty surrounding air and in the glass globes of the oil lamps because the magician from the circus used to cover bottles with a cloth, then whisk it away to reveal clouds of butterflies, his grandmother

—I'm sure I put it somewhere

feeling around in her mouth

—Open your mouth

looking at her askance

—Did you swallow it?

the stain on the shoe annoyed with the screens, where none of the organs are writing sensible sentences, instead of declaring

—I'm working

they make spelling mistakes and go off on a tangent, the pituitary gland speaks of the evenings in the fall when the storks leave, the thymus is missing the blonde foreigner, the blood talks about a bicycle going round and round a chestnut tree, but what's all this nonsense about bicycles and chestnut trees, at which point he leaves in a huff

—I really can't work in these conditions

the presents from the visitors finally forced his hands to offer themselves to themselves, here are some fingers, but what will you do with them, the ten you have are quite enough, a few people irritated by the endless March rain, the seamstress accompanying his mother

—Your son

and his mother, whose lack of teeth befuddled her words

—So many of my people have died

but she doesn't list them, because she can't recall their names, you choose, I don't care, he felt he was being rude, bothering the family and taking up a space to which he had no right, it seemed to him that he existed only intermittently, emerging from a torpor that bore no relation to sleep, someone called out

—Maria Otília

in a garden with a battered old baby carriage at the door and Maria Otília like his Godfather Apolinário a shadow in the mirror, one morning they found the cradle in the attic, a cradle all twisted iron hanging from two hooks, his grandmother

—You spent a year in that

and how strange to have been someone else and then another someone else until he became the man he was today, at five, at seventeen, at forty, at five, a gentleman playing the piano and turning round on his stool

—What do you think?

not noticing the invisible waters that were slowly rising and would soon drown them all, the maid saying to him when he was seventeen

—You're not your father

and obviously he wasn't his father, his dead father, different jars rattling in the pantry, a different packet landing on the floor, his haste

—Help me

and knowing that his grandmother would be sure to tell him off

—How shameful

at forty a sickening sense of pointlessness, a woman by his side and him saying

—Don't leave me

the street door slamming or him inventing that door slamming and suddenly in the living room a precipice into which he was about to fall, the stain on the shoe was telling a group of students about his case while he was thinking about the swallows filling the gaps between gutter and roof with detritus and mud, the amount of trash in the world, my friends, another past, another present, let's leave the trains endlessly coming and going and the swallows, wretched birds, screaming out on my behalf, the seamstress accompanied his mother out into the corridor, he remembered hearing her sing

—What a memory you have

and why are the days composed of episodes like that, the clocks mark the hours one by one but the days go bounding over each other, they go from Saturday to Thursday and from Monday to Friday full of brief intervals our memory has lost, what did we do on Tuesday, what happened on Sunday, perhaps I'll be here in May when the cherry blossom is about to come out, the stain on the shoe

—May is a long way off

and that's the problem, it always is, it never arrives when it should

—If you'd come to see me six months ago

at the time when the beggar with the harmonium was playing on the corner with a beret on the ground for any donations, and there's yet another new past, there was no beggar in his past, the beggar's master picked up the beret, counted the money if there was any or instead of coins only bottle tops, grabbed him by the lapels and carried him off, the beggar

—What's wrong?

picking the feathers off his clothes, they turned left by the Seventh-day Adventist church, attempted to play a fado, retrieved the beret, disappeared among the Tipuana trees and headed for an abandoned ground-floor apartment or a yard or so of fence made of zinc sheeting and the ruins of a mattress and some rags, the sheets in which he was lying in the hospital were rags too, the lights were rags, the pain was a rag in a body of rags, and next month's swallows were rags he would not get to see, he was amazed to feel no surprise or terror, a telephone ringing, not for him, who no longer counted, for some useful person, a nurse, a doctor, as a child he used to hide in the cellar while they looked for him, the cook would let down the bucket into the well, but no one had drowned there, a boot

—At least he's not down there

and him gauging the weight of his absence until the rustling of creatures behind a barrel frightened him and he went upstairs, his grandmother would look at him as she would at his Godfather Apolinário in the mirror, a shadow in a hat and with a little bag of apples for the journey because the dead need to eat, studying the carpets with a sense of endless disappointment

—How old everything is

and don't fall silent, keep talking, as long as you can keep awake, dear God, how still everything is, not even the sound of the cat's tail, his grandmother

—Is that you?

afraid she would be left alone to count the sick people from the tungsten mines waiting out in the square

—There are two missing today

looking around the table at us

—We're all here

weighing herself in the pharmacy

—I haven't become diabetic, have I?

putting down the jar of jam to examine my grandfather

—Fortunately, his color's still good

strolling through the rooms to check we were in bed and putting her ear to our mouths to make sure we were breathing, when she lit the lamps for the saints it wasn't the flame that moved, it was the walls and the ceiling, the world growing sharper in the remaining oil, then burning out with a whiff of wick, his Godfather Apolinário's wife

—You won't inherit a penny

as if she were rich, a small pension, some old furniture, a mug with the handle glued on, and she so proud of that mug

—It's French

she didn't live near the mountains but in a village where she said you could hear the sea when the beech trees created the wind just as the trees create the birds, building them feather by feather inside the leaves, then releasing them, growing plump with the effort, then growing thin again, if they expelled the birds all at once, only the trunk would be left, the stain on the shoe

—I wonder what he's thinking

merely receiving other people's birds and inventing his own, the pain didn't bother him, it was part of life, as were his out-of-synch lungs, on the eve of his operation he felt offended by the tranquillity of the objects that he had chosen and which should be grateful to be living with him, the stain on the shoe

—Let's see what we find

and what the stain on the shoe might find alarmed him, he picked up the phone, put down the phone, went into the kitchen for a drink of water and the faucet splashed him, a child's footsteps in the apartment above, the sound of falling and the neighbor who slit open envelopes with his key reading the mail in the hallway and getting annoyed about the bills, scolding the child, what would it be like to have a son, he felt a draft, unable to comprehend where it could be coming from, given that he'd shut the windows so as to be alone and take the measure of himself, but how if he couldn't even touch himself, he did so with his eyes only, he remembered his grandfather, he remembered his grandmother, but how odd that he didn't remember his father, where are you hiding, I can't find you, he could remember his uncle dragging his suitcase down to the station and the old locomotive where he used to play with the fat boy of the fourteen rivers, whom he had to help up the steps, the sense that his uncle had been crouched there until daybreak and before day broke, when the granite began to come to life through the dogs and the cockerels who would detach themselves from the stone, his uncle returning not to the house but to the well, clinging to the pulley, the fat boy sitting in the driver's seat

—Where shall we go now?

and he who couldn't recall a single river

—To see the Mondego

at least knew a thread of water and a twisted willow tree, his uncle let go of the pulley and not a sound or only the soundless sound that accompanies the void, no postcard *arrive Thursday miss you* and there have been hundreds of Thursdays since then, when the mailman

—He hasn't sent a postcard, he must have forgotten

when he arrived in the ward he handed over his wallet, his money and his watch, they gave him a kind of gown and some sort of slippers and pointed to the bed, where he lay down as he lay down in his own bed when he imagined himself dead and got up a few minutes later glad to have been resurrected, the doctor visited him that afternoon

—We have a little meeting tomorrow

and they did have a little meeting, in a room with vertical lighting like in a boxing ring and him helpless in his nakedness, his grandmother saying to the mailman

—You're not hiding things from me, are you?

his uncle's Christmas presents spent ages

—Perhaps he'll come himself

sitting by the fireplace, the fat boy didn't want to go to the Mondego, he wanted to bound up the mountainside and chase the wolves, the anesthetist invisible in all that whiteness

—Clench your fist

and he clenched his fist, thinking fearfully

—Help

his mother eventually put his uncle's presents on top of the closet, where they grew gray with dust, an undershirt, a pen, a coin purse that closed with a click and that she kept opening and closing, delighted with that click, such simple pleasures bring us so much happiness, taking the tops off beer bottles or scraping off the wax from candlesticks with your fingernail, the fat boy finally compromised with

—OK, the Mondego it is

and they spent hours watching the trains, Senhor Liberto leaving work with his flag under his arm, his wife hoeing the cabbages behind the urinal with the chickens for company, the anesthetist

—I can't find a decent vein

in the hope of being fed some corn, one Saturday every month the dentist would pitch a tent in the square and, a brief parenthesis here, he never forgot the sound of the rain on the canvas, the anesthetist was choosing another blue line and poking and poking, his mother, thinking no one was watching, brought the stepladder the cleaner used and climbed up four steps to the top of the closet and you could hear the click of the coin purse anywhere in the house, when she saw me she pressed her wedding ring to her chest

—You startled me

her heartbeat returning to normal as she struggled to come up with excuses

—I was afraid it might get rusty

meanwhile, the needle was looking for him under his skin, and the noise of the rain on the tent where the laborers' jaws accompanied their one molar, wishing the others would come back, and yet if they kill a colleague over some dispute about irrigation they just stand there waiting for the police jeep to arrive, despite this I caught Virgílio crying with his arms about his mule because it had broken a leg and yet when his daughter died his face was utterly impassive, he even took the spade from the gravedigger and helped bury her and that evening he beat everyone at dominoes in the café, he also remembered the man

—I found the vein, then lost it again

whose leg was crushed by a tractor, his nose became very slightly smaller but however small, his eyebrows closed over it, the pharmacist

—You won't need so many pairs of trousers now

and damn me, but the man with the leg smiled at the joke, he came back months later walking on crutches and sat down on a step to watch the sunset or rather to make the sun set because it was beginning to set in him, his features growing darker and the afternoon imitating him, the first bats emerged from his pockets, the anesthetist

—At last

and him filling the syringe not red as he expected but brown, the coin purse clicking in a nearby room so perhaps he hadn't left the house, soon his grandmother would arrive with plates containing jam and cookies

—Help yourselves

and the maid sprinkling water on the blouses over the sink next to the ironing board, the stain on the shoe came and stood next to him, or was it his father, saying

—You know

very softly, he wanted to tell him about the blonde foreigner by the swimming pool where the pine trees lay down on the surface of the water, but a person wearing a cloth mask said

—Don't speak

and his father stroking his cheek beneath the ringing of the crickets, his house now a dwarf palm tree on the balcony, they mended the pipe on the washbasin and replaced the paintings as he moved farther off from himself down a confused tunnel, the fat boy of the rivers

—Where does the Mondego end?

the bespectacled daughter who would never marry used to help out in the shop and the already solemn son studying to be a priest would inherit the curate's housekeeper, he spotted his grandfather and his newspaper on the balcony, then lost him, he owned nothing, only absences and the pain that went through his body in the briefest of flickers, reminding him of what he wanted to forget, the hospital, the doctors, the gadget on his wrist calculating how long his life would last, his Godfather Apolinário pointing at him and saying to his grandmother

—Are you sure he's a relative of yours?

and him feeling an urge to show him envelopes stuffed full of photos, one of them was of the whole school and he was eighth from the right in the second row, he could recognize himself because his smock was buttoned up the wrong way, even now if he didn't start buttoning from the top and move cautiously downward he still got it wrong, there would always be one too many buttons or one too many buttonholes, the pharmacist's stepson in the middle of the class and his Godfather Apolinário commenting on the dwarf

—Are they really just like us?

yes, piles of photographs, him holding a tennis racket and pretending to play or sitting on the driver's seat, the reins hanging loose, while the animal ate from the nose bag, his lazy tail shooing away flies invisible in the photo, the wedding he didn't talk about, he ended up with the apartment when they shared things out, and when he put the key in the door he could smell traces of what no longer existed and think that, wish that, run his hand over the other side of the bed, he was sitting in his office feeling perfectly relaxed when he heard a sound somewhere that reminded him of the afternoon when, no, forget it, no, go on, the truth, no, forget that too, the stain on the shoe filling in the form and asking his name and age

—Marital status

an awkward pause, *marital status,* what an odd expression, the dwarf was called Afonso, his Godfather Apolinário

—Afonso?

surprised that he had a name, pronouncing it slowly

—Afonso

in a dreamlike slow-motion way and him wanting to defend the dwarf, he had to be called something, what's wrong with Afonso, the pen in the hand of the stain on the shoe suspended motionless over the form was irritating him, he said

—Divorced

as if he were vomiting up an accumulation of misunderstandings, happy days, resentments, the idea that the word *divorced* wasn't enough but why explain, he swallowed what tasted to him like anger and tears and for a moment what did his illness matter, Afonso's little legs swaying his body, his wife didn't phone and didn't come back, they swore to him that she had remarried, and the stain on the shoe saying out loud as he wrote

—Divorced

that night he didn't turn on the light, afraid he might find her on the sofa, he heard the anesthetist

—He's ready

but ready for what, he didn't feel ready for anything, he missed his wife but he wouldn't admit it for all the money in the world, he called out not with his voice but with a prolonged sob

—Maria Otília

his soul incapable of finding its niche and calming down, he couldn't hear the stain on the shoe's questions but the long-drawn-out sob responded on its own, there were two of us, you see, two of us, the nurse

—His temperature's gone up

of course it had, perhaps he really was ready and the circle was closed, she didn't like being called Maria Otília, whenever

—Maria Otília

a frown line would appear, a nostalgia for the source of the Mondego, they left the car, yes I really must be ready, on a side road and clambered through the forest guided by the frogs' furious croaking, so much suffering among the rocks and all for half a dozen drops of water, when the dwarf disappeared the pharmacist fiercely energetically grinding up herbs in a mortar

—He's gone to the city to study

and if only you would let me, Maria Otília, but you won't, sorry, the nurse to the stain on the shoe

—He seems to be in pain

as if it were the pain that was troubling him and it wasn't, it was your absence, Maria Otília, after supper I would stay and watch you putting the dishes and the cutlery away in the machine so that a kind of peace, no, forget it, the stain on the shoe

—There's no point asking him, because he doesn't respond

and how could he respond when he was busy driving the locomotive abandoned on the siding up into the mountains, the owner of the Englishmen's hotel appeared on the balcony and waved, he was sorry not to be able to say good-bye to Virgílio on the bramble-lined path, the bed set off toward the hospital corridor and he thought he saw his uncle getting off the bus, not climbing out of the well, Uncle, what did you do in Spain that made you age so quickly, there must be a village there too, and a church and a curate's housekeeper offering people grapes

—No need to wash them, I don't use sulfates

pinning back two stray locks, Senhor Liberto asking

—What train is that?

a train he hadn't ordered to depart with a wave of his flag, Maria Otília, not just Otília, with the *Maria* augmenting the *Otília,* when he first met her

—Call me what you like, what does it matter what my name is?

unable to find it on the timetable and it wasn't even a train, just a lot of clapped-out connecting rods, his uncle carrying the same suitcase and wearing the same coat, he informed him

—All the Christmas presents from all the Christmases are on top of the closet

but his uncle wasn't even looking, he was looking at the dentist pitching his tent and the rooks flying up, when he opened the door his grandmother

—How did you manage to escape from the mirror?

checking to see if there was mud on his shoes and probably the first swallows had arrived despite the March rain, Dona Lucrécia passing him in the street

—Have you been away?

and him feeling happy in the train because everything was right again, the square, the cemetery, the orchard, the week's dishes in the sink, not in the machine, he would do that on Saturday when he had time, if he had time, the stain on the shoe

—He doesn't seem to be in pain

and I swear not so much as a twinge, he felt good, perhaps the name didn't matter, Maria Otília, her clothes in the closet but he didn't touch her clothes, he had no interest in the past, the fat boy of the fourteen rivers

—When we were young

an eyelid trembling, not her chin, the bespectacled daughter

—Don't make your arteries work too hard

he had been right about the hospital window, swallows, Dona Irene

—It's been ages since I played the harp

and even if she doesn't play the harp we can hear her in the evening, beneath the ever-rustling treetops, a shower of notes.

1 April 2007

Who was that person staring at him, not leaning over the bed but standing very erect beneath the lights that made his hands seem larger, the shadow cast by the hands enormous and on his face a stern expression he didn't understand, no nurse, no doctor, no visitor in the room, only that person looking at him, no episode from the past distracting him from himself, the locomotive, the fat boy, what he had once desired and never had, what he had hoped for and that never came, what he had wanted and had lost, Maria Otília at the window, that is, at the far end of the world, not even thinking about him, and the hope that the swallows would arrive not just in his mind but in his mouth because the word made them real in a way that almost satisfied him, did satisfy him, he had never found a dead swallow, they lived forever and perhaps that was what the person staring at him was criticizing him for, that he wasn't going to live forever, his grandmother lining up the jam jars in one corner of his memory, him listening to his father at the Englishmen's hotel, and his uncle

—I'm not a man

as effortful as moisture seeping from granite, a crack on its face where one expected to see a snake or an insect and instead of the snake or the insect the moisture that took ages to appear, perhaps it was his uncle and not his father whispering

—You know

given that he was getting everything including people muddled up, the conviction that if he did go back to the village he wouldn't recognize it, Dona Lucrécia's chair vanished, the post office building moved elsewhere, Senhor Liberto absent and the trains therefore setting off in impossible directions, trampling through reedbeds and orchards, the person who called him

—Antoninho

grappling with doorknobs that weren't there but refusing to accept that they weren't, give me back what belongs to me and help me continue making sense of the pain, if I lose you, all this is a farce, oxygen, tubes, the catheter in which my body deposits its detritus and the person staring at me in silence, he asked if the sea was above or below the clouds and what did he care about the sea and what was the point of the waves, when he was a child he would focus at random on one wave slowly growing in size

—It's me

and all the waves that followed, the fear of being forgotten obliged him to run over to his mother, who was chatting to the neighbor with the sunshade

—Wait a moment, I'll talk to you in a minute, sweetie

and how could she talk to him if he was nothing, you won't see me again, you know, your son is an ex-wave or an old metal cradle in the cellar, declaring to the person staring at him

—It's over

I was so excited about the swallows but not a sign morning or afternoon, tell me if the sea is above or below the clouds and I won't bother you anymore, I promise, I think it must be above the clouds because I couldn't see it, what was my liver or my heart writing that I couldn't feel, they were remembering Maria Otília drawing away from him when he tried to embrace her

—My God

even though God didn't bother with people, he simply created them

—You can all stay over there if you like

my wave will return after long, long years and I will be a fleck of foam on the crest, he suspected that the person staring at him was himself, how often had he waited with his nose pressed against the window for Maria Otília's shopping bag to appear round the corner, the piano tuner would arrive in the bus to work on Dona Irene's harp and spend hours on one chord, adjusting each string, creating errant melancholies until the timbre filled with life and his uncle, deeply touched, said

—That's exactly how I feel

Maria Otília and her bag never appeared around the corner, the commander's wife, the lady in the little beret who looks after a cousin of hers

—She's no worse, fortunately

the piano tuner's fingers weren't even touching the strings of the harp and yet sounds still emerged, what we want to communicate doesn't need us in order to pronounce that name identical to our secret name, preserved since infancy to protect us from the dark and from the terrible messages that are emitted by the china cabinets and that we alone know, it was hidden from Maria Otília too, he didn't speak it out loud and yet the person watching him knew it, how come you know my name, not

—Antoninho

not

—Antunes

but his real name, he whispered it to the chestnut tree, pressing his lips to the trunk, when they cut down the tree he was afraid the name might escape from beneath the bark but thankfully the chestnut tree said nothing, perhaps the earth drank the name and it's lying buried there among rocks and the skeletons of dogs murmuring a syllable indistinguishable from the speeches made by the wind, the piano tuner would catch the bus beneath a frenzy of notes and he felt sorry for him, for that man who had all the habits of a forgetful widower, a tube of polish with the cap missing, only half the bed slept in and in the other half a void to which he had become as accustomed as he was to the apron on its hook, if asked

—Did that apron belong to your late wife?

he would reply without even looking at it

—I don't know

besides, what would be gained by looking, why did the person staring at him not explain to him if the sea was above or below the clouds, if only the piano tuner could cure his illness instead of the doctor, who didn't even have a wrench and was justifying himself to the visitors

—There's not much we can do

the kidneys, the heart and the liver writing careful, thoughtful speeches on the screen, the cook

—Antoninho

and even if the lips moved, the water pump would cover them, the metal complaining about the filth and the mud, if the sea was beneath the clouds, the waves rising up from the ground were just more gray water, he tried to recall the beach but all he could remember was the drowned man covered by a sheet and how he couldn't bring himself to lift one corner of it and a man in a suit

—Move along

if he had lifted one corner

—Is that Antoninho there?

the piano tuner in the bus under the elm trees in the square blowing his nose in a discreet little arpeggio and because of that arpeggio the entire village widowed, dozens of aprons on hooks, everything orphaned, Dona Irene thinking about him

—Senhor Moreira

not realizing that she's thinking about him, and when she does, rolling down her sleeves and buttoning up her collar

—I must be mad

when it rained, as it did in the hospital ward, the maid with a bit of sacking over her shoulders running out to cover the daffodils, the person staring at him said

—It's true

glad to be able to recover some memories, he must have achieved what his mother wanted and wasn't able to give him, knowing more rivers than the fat boy, a job somewhere other than Lisbon, where her clothes and her hairstyle made her feel like an old lady in a shawl gnawing at a potato in a cave, the nurse crushed up a pill in a spoon so that he could swallow it and his mother

—I look like a penniless old woman, don't I?

without the presence of the mountains to justify the world, what's happened to the rooks, I can't see them, what's happened to the marketplace, the nurse wiping his chin

—Nice boys don't spit out their medicine

the driver turned on the engine and it was the elm trees that were leaving, the bus and the piano tuner still there because he was still a widower, grief lasts a long time, my friends, his mother trying on a ring

—I look even more pathetic like this

and Maria Otília's wedding ring on the tray on the coffin along with a lone earring missing a pearl, he could reconstruct her from that earring if his illness allowed, the bus and the piano tuner marooned forever in the square with no elm trees or pigeons, nice boys don't spit out their medicine, they do as they're told, he went with his mother to the train, where people were cramming big bundles in between the seats along with turkeys in cages, it was probably December, the Savior is born, alleluia, the best china on the table, the best wine, he was never given a gift that he liked because what he wanted was a clown with a ring in its belly and when you pulled the ring you heard guffaws that were at once strident and melancholy and which even now I find troubling, my mother sitting next to a couple of rabbits in a wicker cage, their eyes full of a tenderness as deep as a lake, I'm a nice boy who doesn't spit out his medicine, even though the nurse is wiping my chin

—Ungrateful boy

he was trying to swallow but some cartilage got in the way, his mother was talking to the rabbits, who didn't make her feel quite so pathetic, the stain on the shoe

—However fast these things develop, they still take time

and inside him

—Mom

noticing the word and trying to gather it up before anyone else spotted it, the fleeting suspicion of a swallow right
by the window and the shadow of the bird still there despite
the rain distorting it, he leaned the ladder against the wall
so as to climb up and break the eggs and the ladder buck-
led, the maid

—Antoninho

at the same time as Dona Irene was abandoning her harp

—Nothing seems to come out right

no one was wiping her chin or telling her off for spitting
out her medicine, the guffaws of the clown he had heard in
the shop when the salesman suddenly tugged at the ring

—The things they come up with

those guffaws still troubled him as the doll jiggled about
in its yellow tailcoat, and as soon as the ring reached its belly
again it fell silent with a click, its face utterly impassive,
there was a switchboard operator like that at work whose
soul had been rusted up by life, her features immutable,
what's wrong, Dona Armanda, always the soul of politeness,
he imagined her on Sundays ironing a spotted blouse and
spending the holidays at home counting the daisies on the
wallpaper, she would reach one hundred and eighteen and
realize she'd gone wrong because she'd been distracted by
the sound of the little girl walking around in the upstairs
apartment, she couldn't remember being a child, she remembered a woman

—Take your feet off the armchair

and as the centerpiece on the table the national coat of

arms and the king's crown, a voice belonging to someone she couldn't even imagine

—Careful, Armanda

the nurse examining his diaper

—Nothing there, Doctor

the stain on the shoe studying the diaper

—I'd be surprised if there were

and Dona Armanda searching for the voice and unable to find out where it was coming from, so many voices waiting to be born, she was sure that if she added them up they would also come to one hundred and eighteen, her wristwatch

—Almost five o'clock, how annoying

amazed at the capricious nature of time, I believe in the hands of the clock and I don't believe in them, I'm forty-six years old and I have osteoporosis and a goiter, they told me to drink milk to strengthen my bones

—Look at those blank spaces on the X-ray

and her having no idea what the blank spaces even meant, what she could see were pale spots against a dark background, that's what I'm like under my skin, the stain on the shoe warning the visitors

—His organs are failing

the spleen, the bone marrow, one kidney, the one he still had, the pancreas, whose loyalty positively filled him with pride, his heart, to which he was also grateful, the pain accompanying him

—Don't go away

and him glad of the pain's comforting company

—Let's stick together, my friend

which despite everything, close to extinction, was battling on, if he should spot the sea beneath the clouds from the window, not the wave that had died years ago, other people also rising up like waves to break on the beach and whom no one would remember tomorrow or the day after, the clown's laughter surrounding him with its shrill jubilation, no footsteps in the upstairs apartment, they were trotting around in Dona Armanda's head, her

—Be quiet

and regretting that

—Be quiet

given that they too would grow old and spend Sundays counting daisies and getting it wrong, the woman who told her

—Get your feet off the armchair

joining them

—Why don't I die?

and Dona Armanda at five years old incapable of keeping house, how do you turn on the vacuum cleaner, pay the bills and light the oven, inside the swallow's eggs little bald creatures demanding to exist, the stain on the shoe

—His organs are failing

and the sea beneath the clouds, given that if it was above the earth where would it be, and along with the earth the rivers down which he had set off toward the open sea, one afternoon he gave a frog to his grandmother, and his grandmother, instead of applauding, hid behind the table and closed her eyes

—Take that ugly thing away

and so off he went in search of a pond where he could set it free, what if he could set himself free of the illness, the stain on the shoe

—He's recovered, who would have thought it?

so many nights spent in the hospital, his grandfather's insomnia stumbling on the stairs, his parents' asthma in the second room on the right, where the headboard gradually stopped beating against the wall, the fear that he might be kidnapped and wrapped up in a sheet and handed over to the wolves, he kept saying

—I can't sleep

and suddenly morning and the walls pleated with sounds, the water pump, the cook putting logs into a basket, Virgílio harnessing the mule to the cart and venting his bad temper on the creature with a stick, checking that no wolf had eaten his fingers, it seemed to him that he had three thumbs instead of two, he checked again and there were only two, what a relief, who can guarantee that thieves don't sometimes add things and only pretend to take them away, there were times when he found unexpected objects in the drawers, a nail clipper, receipts, who goes around secretly filling the cupboard with things that aren't ours, who can assure him they didn't put that illness in him just as they put the nail clippers and the receipts in the drawers, the nurse

—Time for your medicine

collaborating with the burglars by stopping him thinking, if his organs were failing how would he protect himself from the others, the pain changed its position, gnawing instead at the back of his neck, the doctor to the visitors

—With the morphine we've given him he can't be in any pain

and him uncertain as to whether he was suffering or not, the person staring at him from immediately beneath the lights

—Of course you're in pain

and yet he couldn't locate the source of the pain, all over his body or somewhere outside, all around him, there were moments when he could feel it moving about on the blanket or sitting on his bedside table waiting, moments when he looked for it in vain because it was heading off down the corridor, imitating the nurses' footsteps, perhaps the telephone in the next room was his pain calling him

—Is Senhor Antunes there?

since they were mere acquaintances, they weighed each other up, skirted round each other and didn't even exchange greetings

—Of course you're in pain

and he really wasn't in pain, honestly, the mosses letting the river trickle through them, he could certainly understand how difficult that was, not like him thinking about the piano tuner waiting in the square and about the turkeys on the train that might end up in Spain or in the well where there's always a drowned man moving about among the slime, you threw in a pebble and no one was there, you didn't throw in a pebble and there he was

—Antoninho

the Antoninho in the hospital with his liver and its pompous speeches beginning to run out of words

—His organs are beginning to fail one by one

even though he could still understand it by summarizing sentences that would soon seem rather absurd, one syllable, two syllables like the turkeys, spoken in fits and starts, what's going on, send me packing, you surely don't want to cook me, Maria Otília, a bit of shoulder that I don't need, the tongue that gets in the way of my gums, I speak with my teeth and I don't have all of them, you can see the spaces, the space left by the chestnut tree a hole and no earth to cover it, they smooth it over with the spade and a week later the hole is back, why don't they plant another chestnut tree to disguise how much they miss it, dozens of chestnuts crushed between two stones, the maid

—Mind you don't get colic, dear

and me with my stomach all bloated vomiting up myself in an attempt to bring up my guts and with them the nausea and the colic, my grandmother

—Those green chestnuts would make any boy ill

more dangerous than the stuff they kill cockroaches with or the sulfate they put on the vines, the bottle with a skull on the label, keep out of reach of children, he picked up the bottle, containing an apparently inoffensive liquid, to drink or not to drink, he unscrewed the lid, put the bottle to his lips, saw the skull, whose eye sockets swallowed him whole, and quickly put the top back on, terrified, if those eyes were to swallow him what would happen then, as for his teeth, a man in a white coat

—Those eyeteeth will have to come out

and the man in the white coat tipping them into a bucket

—Only another eleven to go

I imagine the piano tuner was still waiting in the square, convinced he was about to go back to town, given that the driver was at the wheel

—We'll be there in a couple of hours

with him maneuvering the gears of the broken-down tractor, imagining that the tractor would move and scare off the rooks, Dona Lucrécia, who knew about the mystery of immovable things that move when they say good-bye

—Boy

she didn't say good-bye, because she considered herself to be eternal, look, once and for all, what do we think, is the sea above or below the clouds, who bends over the water pump to bring in the waves, who regulates the tides and invents the silence that almost doesn't exist at the moment when the foam evaporates and we discover a calendar that teaches fish about years

—Do you know what a week is, do you know what a month is?

and there are no weeks or months, there are layers of monotony that would bore him to death in the desolation of winter, how else could one cope with January except by putting a cross through each number, eager to keep turning the pages, the next morning we ask

—What's the date today?

and each little cross is an eternity because not so much as an hour has passed, we thought that it was night but the night doesn't exist, that we were sleeping when we were wide awake, his grandmother sipping the evening tea that the pharmacist recommended for her nerves, his father

—You know

spoken on just one occasion, which he believed had been many, many occasions, the blonde foreigner always about to leave, the stain on the shoe

—If we could only know what was going on inside his head

and they couldn't, of course, they had never seen the blonde foreigner or the piano tuner, and there was always the nagging doubt as to whether he had actually seen them or just dreamed them up, no visitor in the room to distract him, the stain on the shoe

—People will always be a mystery

but there's no mystery, people are the same as beetles and cows, beetles fly into the lamp on the porch and get burned and cows get the shakes for a day or two, then fall shaking to the ground, where they stop shaking and are buried, and only then do we realize with a shock how big they are, they don't chew grass, they chew patience, the grass is just a front, just as today I'm eating nothing but patience, if he needed an arm he wouldn't have one, or a leg, because there wasn't one, but the pulse in his wrist continued to push him onward even though there was no onward, only the wall getting closer and closer and nothing behind it except his grandmother

—Goodness, you've grown thin

looking for the sugar to make an eggnog or a little glass of anisette

—Have you stopped eating, child?

he was back home, glad to be out of hospital, I'll put the weight back on, don't worry, I won't get any thinner, the stain on the shoe saying

—Come back and see us

a good-luck ribbon around his wrist, do you believe in such nonsense, Doctor, charm bracelets, horseshoes, enamel four-leaf clovers, his uncle

—Where have you been, boy?

and he couldn't bring himself to say that he'd been ill in the hospital, the chestnut tree helped him out with a murmur of raindrops

—Oh, here and there

and he really had been here and there, with the pain gnawing his bones and his diapers unsoiled, the first swallow on the balcony roof, the second on the beam in the barn, his grandmother

—You frightened us

and him watching the March drizzle, the nurse with the medicine

—Sit up a bit, will you, my friend

they just have to lift him up from the pillow, the nurse wiping his chin

—He's spilled more than half the medicine

just as more than half of the Mondego spilled over onto the grass, Maria Otília on the one afternoon she went with him into the mountains smoothing his lapels

—Look at the state of you

and a snake, bees, wolves crouched and drooling, the child

—Bread, bread

while above the clouds the sea, out of the rain, intact, with a steamship reduced to just a funnel, smoke, and once the smoke had vanished, the horizon, none of the ceiling lights bothered him, his grandmother

—I'm going to turn out the light now, so go to sleep

smoothing the sheets, tucking in the blanket, then tiptoeing out as if her slippers were toes

—He was exhausted, poor love

and an echo from the well, a shudder of the curtains, what might be a stretcher slipped past nearby but there was no one else apart from the piano tuner, adjusting a final peg in his chest, trying out an arpeggio and saying to Dona Irene

—He's ready.

2 April 2007

Someone has died in the hospital, either him or someone else, because there are more voices in the corridor, more footsteps, and the door was closed with a hurried *Excuse me,* giving him the impression that no one would open it again, he was left alone with no pills and no visitors, when he was little his mother would sing as she sat at her sewing machine and he would watch as her fingers propelled the cloth along, mopeds waiting on the edge of the pine forest with the miners' children, who collected the resin, why is the blood of trees so slow and neither red nor chestnut brown but white, there must be more worlds inside us but if there are who lives in them, because he hasn't seen them, someone must have died because there are dozens of creatures in the hospital, although he was beginning to believe he was alone, the lady in the yellow gown who raised the blind in the morning saying to some patient or other

—Oh Dona Lurdes, Dona Lurdes, you've spilled your tea

and Dona Lurdes's apologies were an embarrassed thread of words, at least the Dona Lurdes who was there with him, presumably beneath the same lights and the same rain on the windowpanes and expecting the same future swallows, unless it was just some trick to fool him and a woman was pretending to be the lady in the yellow gown and another woman was pretending to be Dona Lurdes, not a drop of tea, not one jot of consideration, little mocking giggles, if he turned his head he would see them nudging each other

—Silly fool

not realizing that they didn't fool him, he must ask the person staring at him to send a note to Virgílio and the cart waiting for him downstairs, how far is it from Lisbon to the village, how long would it take to travel from the hospital to home, scattering potatoes along the road as they went, Virgílio's back rather than his mouth saying

—Don't worry, we'll get there

and the pain was left in the empty room so that the doctor could distribute it to the other patients, you can't leave the hospital with it, there isn't enough for everyone, when you're discharged they check your pockets

—Where's that little pain?

adding

—You'll be charged for how much pain you felt

perhaps he would be charged for the swallows too, and the fear of dying costs a fortune, he even owed them for the rain, the man in charge of the clouds asking his colleague

—How many quarts of rain for bed eleven?

the colleague looking in his notebook

—At least one and a half, but I'll have to check the hygrometer

and since he didn't need the rain, what would he do with the drops he hadn't used and what if he wasn't even given any drops, a barely noticeable dampness, one afternoon his grandfather emerged from behind his newspaper and there was some dampness beneath his lower eyelid too, how did you manage that, you who can't even hear the chestnut trees or the insects in the vineyard, it's possible he can hear himself, but what's he saying, his grandmother translated the silence for him

—He wants some more stew

and then I understood that the Mondego was a very difficult melancholy struggling to express itself, they call that a river and we set off along it, hopefully heading for the sea when there is no sea, pine trees, a desire to meet Dona Lurdes and ask purely out of politeness

—What are you going to die of?

and her daughter answering for her

—It's a problem with her aorta

Dona Lurdes's teeth all idle, useless, her nose a tooth sniffing as it randomly bites the air, bite the air, Dona Lurdes, bite yourself, devour yourself while your daughter holds your arm, leaving the sleeve behind, would you like me to help you devour yourself just as I am devouring myself, I've already eaten the cartilage that moves under my skin when they hand me my medicine

—A nice little pill for a nice little boy

and the nice little boy accepting that it is the role of nice little boys to accept and not disobey orders, he had enough money saved up for two or three swallows, although things do get tight at the end of the month, don't give him a whole flock, his grandfather from behind his newspaper

—And now?

and now go and amuse yourself by strolling in the vineyard and keep lining up the pictures by measuring the space between the frames and the furniture, making a mark in pencil so as to get it just right, when he made a mistake, he would wet a finger, leaving a smudge instead of a mark, his grandmother

—At least it keeps him occupied

but it didn't keep him occupied, because his gestures were so soulless, in each of them a

—What now?

once he had finished lining up the paintings he would gaze at them as if asking what are you doing here, what am I doing here, I may be exaggerating because I can't really remember him, I can see the pencil, I can see the paintings, the one with the shipwreck, the one with the horses, the one with the white kitten and the black kitten playing with a ball of wool, I can see my grandfather saying

—Good night

not to us, to someone who looked after him when he was small, reassuring him

—I won't go away

not leaving his bedside, staying with him until he fell asleep, and who if he woke in the night was there in the darkness, his grandmother

—I swear there's a creature with us in the room

and there really was a creature, sitting between the balcony and the closet and which she presumed was a woman but quite who, a relative, a godmother or a nanny she didn't know he'd had and if he did there wasn't even an old photograph of her, she didn't ask

—Who let her in?

because it was clear that his grandfather used to open the back door when she was at mass, she asked Senhor Liberto if he'd seen the creature at the station and Senhor Liberto made a circular motion with his flag

—No one's arrived here for weeks
the pharmacist shooing away ghosts
—That's impossible
Virgílio offended
—There were potatoes in the cart
in other words, the whole world was conspiring against
him and still there was a voice from a different age like the
voice in the house where eighty years ago the factory owner
had committed suicide and which even the old ladies were
afraid to enter, a house with little balconies and chipped mo-
saic panels, the countryfolk used to cross over to the other
side of the road so as not to walk in the shadow cast by the
house, knowing that death was waiting in the attic, a piece
of rope hanging from a roof beam and watercolors of people whose bodies had long since ceased stirring even in the
cemetery, his grandmother a little girl peering into the garden until her mother, greatly alarmed
    —Come away from there
    because the person approaching is covered in animal
hair and walks on all fours up in the mountains or emerges
from behind a bush to stand barefoot before us begging
    —Bread, bread
the stain on the shoe
    —After a certain point the mind starts to wander
    and it's true, it does, the mind doesn't suffer, it simply
loses interest, it doesn't care, it goes slightly mad, thinks the
hospital is a house, plans to leave as if it were easy to leave,
no one leaves, not even us healthy ones, we acquire roots assuming we'll have to move on and that if we move on then
everything will move on with us, my wife or the bank loan I
didn't manage to pay off, the man at the counter

—Another two months, sir, and we'll have to send in the bailiffs

my father clearing his throat

—You'd better not get your clothes dirty

except with my father this was said with slow disdain

—And the fellow wants to be a doctor

many years later, the stain on the shoe was in charge of the ward at the time when his father's prostate had started to multiply, and the stain on the shoe tried to help him only to receive the same disdain

—What do you know about illnesses?

not his frail old father, but his father from earlier days, he remembered him trimming his nasal hairs with a tiny pair of scissors, which he wiped clean on his trousers before presenting his ears to his wife

—Make sure you get every hair

his wife up to her shoulders in two black holes

—If you fidget, I'll hurt you

even safe in a drawer in the cemetery, with half a dozen carnations in a metal vase, his father continued to persecute him

—I bet you kill any of the poor unfortunates you get your claws into

and yet he was one of those unfortunates whom the stain on the shoe had got his claws into, an unexpected pain in his buttock, a kind of dizziness, a kind of nausea, the nurse, not the usual one, a swarthy fellow, holding up his diaper

—Blood

and the swallows had still not arrived, in March perhaps, not in April, when his grandmother would announce

—The swallows have arrived

and the ivy on the walls of the house would become covered in horseflies, why do you get so excited about the swallows arriving, Grandma, they build filthy nests, leave their droppings on the steps, make a real mess, as soon as the stain on the shoe

—Mucus and blood

his father from his drawer in the cemetery retorted fiercely

—And what would you know about that?

if he could control his temper, he would say

—Just leave me in peace, will you, Dad?

hoping that the hairs in his ears would continue to grow, with his mother safe in another drawer and with no scissors to hand, the pain in his buttock extended to his knee, flickered down his tibia, stopped, what a drag, swallows, waking up with wings beating and then with a start

—The factory owner called me

walking over to the rope dragging a chair, climbing onto the chair, adjusting the knot, kicking away the chair and no more illness, no stain on the shoe

—After a certain point the mind starts to wander

his grandmother, his mother and the blonde foreigner at the Englishmen's hotel all gone, a tennis ball bouncing over the fence, don't tread on the shadow cast by the house because I'll come trotting down the corridor covered in animal hair or else appear suddenly round a corner

—Bread, bread

with very long claws and the rump of a wolf, my grandmother discovering me on all fours in the living room

—What the hell's going on here?

nothing's going on, it's just me, I strangle people, go away, the stain on the shoe overcome by his father when he thinks of the drawer containing a small box, his mother sitting at the sewing machine singing and when I hear her the pain diminishes and my heart slows, the stain on the shoe's father from behind his half-dozen carnations

—I assume you at least take a bath now?

the factory owner's patent leather boots weary of swaying a few inches or so above the ground

—You were born centuries after me

curious to find out how the human race has evolved or not evolved, his wife struggling to do up the bodice intended to flatten her rolls of fat

—Oh, Mateus

and Senhor Mateus seeing what life is like and not liking what he sees

—I can't stand this wretched life a moment longer

he took the bookkeeper by surprise and left her to adjust her clothing, his son in the Merchant Navy transporting camphor chests, which is what grows on the waves now, the way eucalyptuses grow in the village, his daughter married to an agronomist, counting the spoons in the cutlery drawer, keeping jealous watch over her inheritance

—There are two missing, Mom

but there weren't just two missing, there were five, who's been meddling with the silverware, someone has died in the hospital, either him or someone else, because there are more voices in the corridor, more footsteps, and the door was closed with a hurried *Excuse me,* giving him the impression that no one would open it again, he was left alone with no pills and no visitors, once during supper he asked his uncle

—Aren't you a man?

his grandmother torturing her napkin and his mother pinching him hard under the tablecloth, Senhor Mateus found the rope in the last chest of camphor his son brought back, Chinese figures in skirts leading hunchbacked buffalo, when they closed the mine the Englishmen vanished and the hotel began to crumble from top to bottom, chimneys sagging and the roof losing its feathers, the stain on the shoe considered changing the flowers placed on the drawer in the cemetery and putting some yellow roses there instead but he was afraid that the urn might say

—Idiot, fancy choosing yellow roses

and so instead of yellow roses, violets, his grandmother pointing at the newspaper

—Does your grandfather seem a bit odd to you?

but he didn't seem odd, it was just that he barely spoke except for a

—Good night

addressed to a relative, a godmother, the nanny his grandmother didn't know he'd had and if he did there wasn't even an old photograph of her, and if he woke up she would be there in the darkness, his grandmother

—I'm sure there's some creature in the room with us

and there really was, a female creature, she presumed it was a woman because from time to time his grandfather

—Adelina

would open the back door when she was at mass, the father of the stain on the shoe with dozens of prostates and his memory escaping off into private regions, where an elderly lady would open a book full of pictures with words underneath, *Tree, Horse, Church, Egg, Bear*

—What's wrong with letting your mind wander, don't you ever do that?

inside the drawer relearning vowel sounds, Senhor Liberto at the station

—No one has arrived in weeks

the timetable dissolving on the wall and the one o'clock fast train not stopping, deserted, we're all here apart from your grandson in the hospital in Lisbon lit by three lamps and waiting for a continuous line to appear on the screens, the nurse hesitating over whether to remove the tubes, the chaplain with a drop of oil

—We're too late, but it won't do him any harm

no one has arrived for weeks, so only old ladies in shawls, the occasional chicken strutting across the square, propelled along by its neck, and Virgílio's cart on the bramble-lined path, the father of the stain on the shoe abandoning the vowels

—I assume you at least know how to read?

and the smell of the path calming him, he was six, perhaps seven years old, he would watch the rooks in the garden shooting sideways glances at him and speaking ill of him, speaking ill of the entire universe with the exception of the sacristan, who left them crusts of bread, hoping he could add a rook to his rice at lunchtime, he tried to find out if they nested in an elm tree, on the ground or in scrub in the mountains among the dilapidated shacks, he went as far as the mimosas where the rocks begin, but stopped, afraid, the stain on the shoe looking around him to check if the nurses had heard him

—Yes, I think I do

not that the ribbon on his wrist would protect him from

his father, and he felt angry with the ribbon, if he had a pen-knife handy he would cut it off, press down on the pedal of the trash can and throw away that useless bit of ribbon, the factory owner came up the steps from the cellar in his patent-leather boots, the left one creaking and the right one silent, what's wrong with that boot, as he crossed the kitchen he felt moved by the nape of the cook's neck with its smell of trees, and the factory owner fighting against the lure of that smell and writing farewell notes in the little room where another camphor chest confirmed his decision, all those Chinese people in skirts on the lid, all those hunchbacked buffalo in rice paddies, the calligraphy as difficult as the heart's calligraphy on the screen, he glimpsed his wife wrestling with the corset crushing her ribs and the nape of the cook's neck returned for a few seconds, although with no smell this time, on the second floor the room with the purple valances where they would receive the bishop, and the factory owner not examining the curtains but examining himself

—I can't stand this wretched life a moment longer

while his daughter was meticulously counting the silver-ware with her beady eyes, every tray, every sugar bowl, every candlestick, and her husband noting down the china in his book

—Are the Limoges ashtrays all there?

the factory owner

—Oh, Mateus

and that

—Oh, Mateus

decided him, he tested the strength of the beam but didn't cry out, because in the hospital people don't cry out, they study your body to see what's wrong with it, his mother used to sing at her sewing machine and he was singing along with her in the ward, he could remember some words but not others, when he didn't remember, he would hum the tune, for example he knew Come and see the beautiful boat but his mother almost never sang that, *Come and see the beautiful boat in which Our Lady is going to put to sea, see the angels rowing,* pious words that pleased his grandmother, do you remember the beautiful boat?

—I'm too old for that, child

but how old was she, she could feel the changing seasons in the water in her bones

—It must be fall, because I've got a cramp in my leg

a slipper dragging along, his grandfather

—Adelina

and her

—Adelina?

Reaching her fingers into the chest of memories but finding no Adelina, just some artificial tulips, a flashlight with no batteries, Senhor Castelo, who could produce coins out of his nose

—I never imagined you were so rich

he would hold his clenched fist to her face and when he opened it there was a handful of loose change, she tried to do the same on her own but it didn't work, Senhor Castelo would offer her one of the smallest coins and bury the others in his pocket

—I don't want you to get too rich

he didn't give them to her, he robbed her, she thought the money must tickle when it came out of his nose, but no, easy as pie, if she could produce money like that she would buy a copper swan at the market with a neck resembling the hooks on clothes hangers and a wart at the base of its beak, his grandfather already ill and saying not to her but to an invisible woman

—Don't leave me

in a voice identical to that of the beautiful boat but without mangling the words, the pharmacist

—Adelina?

and on his grandfather's face what might have been a smile, the nurse in the hospital

—The rascal looks rather pleased with himself

after his grandfather died there was the shape of a body on one side of the mattress, which intrigued his grandmother, while Senhor Liberto with his flag rolled up and tucked under his arm

—There have never been any more passengers, Senhora

given that either there were no trains or they didn't stop there, clouds of steam with no cars and a whistle coming from nowhere that made the pine trees shiver, the bus was still in the square with the piano tuner assuming he was already heading off down the road, the stain on the shoe unable to decide between violets and roses, fearing the wrath of his father

—Flowers are for sissies

outraged by the scent, are there more worlds inside our world and if there are who lives in them, there are moments when you can feel presences, the jug at night pouring out water, you go down to the kitchen and the mug is empty, traces that the hands leave when they touch things, are there more people in the hospital or is he the only one and Dona Lurdes a mere pretense, how could he have been so stupid as to let them operate on him, the father of the stain on the shoe

—You mean you believed my son?

they fiddled the test results, they introduced pain into his body via the intravenous drip, and what did those spots on the X-ray prove, you get lots of spots on photographs, the pain didn't belong to him, they forced him to buy it, the hospital employee

—How much pain would you like this week?

taking swallows out of the cardboard boxes and clipping their wings, and get rid of this problem with my spine because that isn't mine either, they off-loaded it onto me for next to nothing, unlike the spring, which cost a fortune, the nurse holding him down on the pillow

—Don't make me hurt you, my friend

it seemed to him that a thrush, no, not a thrush, a petal stuck to the windowpane, the factory owner tied the rope to the beam, first one knot, then another, he tugged hard, doubled it over, placed his full weight on it to see if it held, made a noose and checked that it tightened smoothly, then put it around his neck

—Oh, Mateus

perfect, the hospital employee to his colleague

—Normally, half a dozen swallows is enough

someone has died in the hospital, either him or someone else, because there are more voices in the corridor, more footsteps, and the door was closed with a hurried *Excuse me,* giving him the impression that no one would open it again, he was left alone with no pills and no visitors, the factory owner remembering the nape of the cook's neck and his wife's hideous corset

—I can't stand this wretched life a moment longer

just like him in the ward because everything was rebelling now, lungs, esophagus, something pulsing in his belly, his grandmother as a little girl peering into the garden until her mother, greatly alarmed

—Come away from there

because the person approaching is covered in animal hair and walks on all fours up in the mountains or emerges from behind a bush to stand barefoot before people, begging

—Bread, bread

monotonously on and on, the stain on the shoe to the visitors he couldn't see, he could see his grandfather

—Adelina

the stain on the shoe

—After a certain point the mind starts to wander

and with his brain wandering the factory owner tightened the noose, he heard

—Oh, Dona Lurdes, Dona Lurdes, you've spilled your tea

and a mocking laugh that stopped abruptly, to be replaced by the rustling of the ash trees.

3 April 2007

Believe it or not, and you clearly don't, well, we haven't seen each other for years, I'm the one who used to leave the towel draped any old how over the towel rail and you used to get annoyed with me and put it straight

—Don't you even know how to do that?

I would promise to fold it neatly and then forget, just as I would promise to turn off the faucets properly only for a drop of water to suddenly startle the world, and I'd promise not to leave magazines on the floor but instead to pile them up on the coffee table, and that's because when I did that it felt like I was living in a doctor's waiting room, and then I remembered the trains and I smiled, there has to be something in life to make me smile, sometimes when we look back at the past we smile as if the past had been a happy place, you

—What are *you* laughing at?

and I was enjoying looking at the me I was back then, not just at the trains but at the Saturday markets, the van belonging to the guy selling boots and me standing entranced before them, my mother tugging at me

—Your boots will last you another year at least

meanwhile buying a dress for herself in the clothes shop

when the one she was wearing would have lasted her another year at least, you may not believe me, but I spent tonight with you, Maria Otília, my mother holding the dress up to herself in the mirror full of stains and squashed insects, not to mention the defects in the glass that made her body all wonky, measuring the shoulders against her shoulders, checking the length of the hem and raising one leg, making me think that the dress would certainly last another year but not her shoes, she would have to give them to the cook, on whose feet they would remain for ages because poor people's shoes, however misshapen, are eternal, they go from being shoes to slippers, from slippers to flip-flops and from flip-flops to ruins, you may not believe me, but I spent tonight with you, Maria Otília, and there I am smiling at the trains, me in the middle of the bed where the nurses put me and me hoping you would touch me, and you on the very edge of the mattress hoping I wouldn't touch you, and I didn't touch you, so that you wouldn't repel me with an exasperated elbow

—Can't you sleep?

while the clothes salesman praised the quality of the fabric, every drip from the faucet a thundering boom and your fingers knocking over the alarm clock as you reached to turn on the light

—Will you never learn?

the crucifix inhibiting me, my trousers sliding off the chair and your blouse perfectly behaved, footsteps in the corridor, the voice amplified by the tiled walls

—He'll be the death of me

footsteps again, the bed rocking

—Frankly

the crucifix and the blouse gone, a whirlwind of sheets above my head

—Good grief

an ominous silence seething with impatiences and yet tonight even though you don't believe me I could almost smell you, not your perfume, your skin, mingled with the acrid smell of urine on my skin, then two or three of my fingers flexed, or I imagined they did, now that I try to flex them I know I only imagined it, I noticed your throat when your sleep changed speed, replacing one dream with another, just as the fridge compressor changed speed as it leaped over some inner alleyway, the boots at the market had a whiff of living animal about them, mine had a whiff of my grandmother's prayer book, and in Maria Otília's dreams a perpetual

—I can't bear it

with no room for me, and the nurse didn't see you when she gave me my medicine, my mother pointing out a stain on the dress to the man in the shop

—What's that?

and he responded at once

—Oh, that's nothing

meanwhile, a damp brush was scrubbing away at the neck of a bottle, there's my grandmother at the jewelry counter and me pleased that the past continues to exist, thus saving me from the precipice at the edge of the mattress, a little boy was doing somersaults on a mat while his one-armed uncle begged for alms, if I were in charge of the hospital room I can guarantee you that all the towels would be properly folded over the rail, except that there were no towels, a washbasin with no dripping faucets, just a bottle of purple soap, from which now and then a sticky paste oozed onto the basin, and no curtains, no paintings, no chess game with one of the pawns sporting an imitation cut-glass head and a little ball of glue harder than the chess pieces, the wind set the church bells ringing and then fell silent, what would I say to the wind if I had the chance, whole pages, books, an endless encyclopedia, and there would still be shirts flapping about on the line and the trunk of a pine tree that fell, scattering the rooks, the nurse returned the next day with a new pill and a new intravenous drip, accompanied by the barber's indecision

—Is it worth treating him?

not realizing that I wasn't there, I was at the market learning to do somersaults, they're not interested in me since I stopped eating green chestnuts, the pharmacist studying my tongue, where all misfortunes are concentrated

—He's as strong as a horse

even though all the horses he knew were sick, what is it about me that irritated you, Maria Otília, apart from the towels and the dripping faucets, the way I spat out fish bones onto my fork as if bestowing a long kiss, my shoes left next to the television, toe to toe in silent accusation, a couple of horses trotting about the field at the mercy of the creatures in the mountains who would soon take them away, they put a piece of rope around their necks and dragged them off up the hill through the prickly gorse, I feel better now, one of my shoulders twitched and I almost managed to spot a swallow, well, not a whole swallow, half a tail and a wing, that's what would happen in the village, they would gather together little by little and suddenly there they all were, forming a perfect line on the roof, ready to shit on us, the maid would destroy their nests of straw mixed with earth and dead butterflies and caterpillars, the birds flying around colliding with the granite, my right shoulder twitched then as if about to make a gesture, and soon I'll be trotting around better than the skin-and-bone horses those hairy hill creatures would conceal in caves, their villages like candles burning down, and me at peace, yes, at peace for the first time since I arrived in the ward, the walls at peace and the lights at peace, I was floating about in the room between Lisbon and the mountains with a flock of raucous crows flying off, the tubes didn't bind me, the lines on the screens didn't hold me back and death was impossible, it must be morning because there's the muffled sound of a vacuum cleaner and the cook busily working the rusty pump, the last Saturday I went there the man who owned the haberdashery shop

—I knew your grandparents

whom I reinvented in the hospital and then lost, the meadow replaced by corn, the bramble-lined path a street of emigrants with china lions, the pharmacy bigger now, the dates of the deceased ever more remote, it's odd how people stay dead for such a long time, they should give up lying still and come back to the places where they used to live and feel the same sense of astonishment that I do and where they too would get lost, Maria Otília was staring at the mirror examining her roots, looking for gray hairs

—I'll never get old

and somewhere or other she will be getting old, chasing black hairs with a fan now because of the hot flashes and the medicine she takes for her ulcer, the only cure for ulcers isn't drinking that stuff, it's cutting off the two corners marked in blue with the miniature saw you find among the folds of the instruction leaflet hidden in the packaging, a small recompense for growing old, opening the vials and finding a yellow stain in a drop of water that you stir not with a spoon but with a knife handle

—I knew your grandparents and your mother before she was married

not mentioning my father in the Englishmen's hotel, the owner of the haberdashery shop knew my grandparents and my mother before she was married, I knew a sewing machine, newspapers, a jacket left on the balcony and jars of peach jam, the storks will arrive along with the swallows, the thrushes, the dinosaurs and the summer insects, if, right now, someone were to give me a bit of mica I would roll it around in the palm of my hand while I gazed out at the neglected vineyard and the henhouse, where the abandoned chickens with no corn to eat were killing one another, the stain on the shoe

—He's starting to give up

and even if I were quietly giving up, I would talk to you for hours if I could talk, and even if I couldn't I would hope to be heard, the nurse to his colleague

—Did you hear something?

and me, just like my grandfather pointing at the pine trees

—What do they want from us?

and behind the pine trees Dona Irene's harp and the piano tuner sitting quite still in the bus, why doesn't he just give me a quick tweak with his wrench and cure me, the man in the clothes shop dismissing the stain and hiding a smaller one that my mother hadn't spotted

—I don't have any benzene, but benzene will get rid of it

who can guarantee that instead of operating they didn't just rub me with benzene while my one-armed uncle begged for alms from the anesthetist, no old lady in a shawl because they put a rope around her neck and led them all off into the mountains, my mother before she was married going for walks with her friends, Clotilde, Júlia, and Alda, who married a soldier, all of them blind now

—I can see a little bit

Alda with her memory gone

—Who was I married to?

and a niece getting annoyed

—If she can't keep the food in her mouth I'll end up sticking a funnel down her throat

Alda rummaging around in the shards of her memory

—What's a funnel?

full of words that have lost all meaning, *basin, saucepan, doorstep,* what does *doorstep* mean

—Lift your foot up onto the doorstep

and Alda still not lifting her foot

—Doorstep?

struggling to translate, her niece lifting her foot for her

—Oh, for heaven's sake

if anyone asked for her name she would hesitate, still anxiously searching in her mind for doorsteps and not finding them, the haberdashery shop a clutter of dusty bits and bobs

—No one's interested in us anymore

days on end spent alone like me in this bed with the same furious desire to leave and yet incapable of leaving, our visitors leave, if I had a son then he might not, no, if I had a son he would leave like all the others, what's the use of a father like him, and perhaps that's what my father meant when he sat staring at the lichens on the wall or my grandfather leafing through the newspaper on the balcony indifferent to the news, my grandmother

—He always was very distracted

but it wasn't distraction, it was life's lack of coherence, the blood in my diaper worries me, I'd rather they put a rope around my neck and drag me off up to the caves, the stain on the shoe

—Here we are, Senhor Antunes

and here we are or rather here I am or rather here is the Senhor Antunes someone will throw a sheet over, the owner of the haberdashery shop

—I knew your mother before she was married

and Alda thinking about that funnel, the pain has come back and installed itself at my waist, not a smooth spherical pain but one full of wrinkles and bumps, almost underneath my skin and very deep, it bothers me without consuming me, cuts into me while leaving me intact, lingers but somewhere far off, I don't know why I feel grateful and yet I do feel grateful to have it, it must be the piano tuner's wrench squeezing a nerve and tightening it to create endless sharps and the sharps are at the base of my cranium, I think I'm using the right term, yes, susurrating, everything white, illuminated, tranquil, not the white of the walls or the white of the lights, a kind of stainless suffering, a pain that reminds me of the burning salty mud the sea leaves behind as it retreats, I wonder, would the pain go away if I did a figure eight around the chestnut tree, if I caught the train or if I rode in Virgílio's cart, given that there must be other bramble-lined paths, brambles are one thing we're never short of here, no, we're certainly never short of brambles or hunger, Clotilde,

Júlia, Alda, who married a soldier, and my mother before she was married, thrilled to be pronouncing their names, used to go out with the grandson of the municipal tax inspector, she hadn't yet met my father

—How old were you when you met Dad?

and her working backward from the date of the big fire in the mountains

—Nineteen

the stain on the shoe

—At this stage of the illness he can't be in any pain

my father, born in the city, following my mother into the square and my mother laughing at his beret

—He was so comical, your father

Clotilde

—He fancies you

my mother not even looking round

—What an awful thought

angry when her friends agreed with her, there was my father, standing underneath the elms, taking off his beret, too shy to speak, everything got tied up on his tongue, words and spit, he choked, coughed, tripped on a stone and staggered over to embrace a tree trunk, whose bark made a hole in his shirt, Júlia

—Have you ever seen such a clown?

the owner of the haberdashery shop

—I remember her wedding too

and my mother didn't feel sorry for the clown but instead a strange emotion

—Who's going to darn his shirt?

curious to ask the stain on the shoe

—How did you treat your wife?

and the stain on the shoe spent every day at the cinema trying to chat up the girl selling tickets

—I could kick myself for doing that

when he knew only her blouse and the hand holding out his change through an opening in the glass

—Aren't you fed up with that movie?

a pious story about Christians and lions, a penance of thirty matinees, almost a whole Lent spent waiting at the exit and why, not out of love, when the lights went up in the auditorium there was just him and an elderly lady still sound asleep, the ticket girl was fatter than he imagined and had something wrong with her leg, and of course the benzene didn't remove the stain, my mother concealed it with a pleat, and the man in the clothes shop

—You obviously didn't rub hard enough

offering her a discount on a skirt for a flamenco dancer with picadors on it, the pain suddenly spread to his bladder, if the illness had been in his urethra instead of his intestines he would be impotent, what a drag, but maybe then he wouldn't be so cocksure of himself, he understood now about the uncle caught between Spain and the well

—I'm not a man

leaving the room clean, the bed made, the books lined up on the shelves and the desk empty, three drawers on either side of the space for his knees, one drawer with the brass handle hanging off because a screw came loose, he had to press down on the top of the drawer and use his fingers to pry it open, the father of the stain on the shoe to the girl at the ticket office, in a voice filled with infinite pity

—Did no one explain to you what my son is like?

his grandmother looked everywhere, inside her foot warmer, in the mattress stuffing, on the bedside table where her slippers were placed one on top of the other to make room for the chamber pot with the chipped enamel handle

—He didn't leave any message for us, not a word?

while a swallow practically intact, lacking only its head and therefore silent, brushed past the hospital window, proving that April was taking shape, his uncle possibly in Spain, given that the well was quiet, any drowned man in the mud made the frenzied movements of someone who cannot find his place among the sharp stones and the empty cans and the impulse to resurface

—I've changed my mind

looking for the hoe before heading for the garden, the pain circling his urethra

—I'm still a man

his pride preserved, it was odd that he couldn't recall a single haberdashery shop in the village, in its place was the shed for the mule and the doubt that his mother had ever not been married, his oldest memory was of falling asleep on her lap, not completely, but plunging in and then resurfacing to the sound of his grandmother clearing her throat, which made him cry because it was preventing him from disappearing into that warm, lacy comfort and forcing him to be himself and he didn't want to be himself, he wanted to be part of that throat, those arms, the nape of the neck that his hand was clasping and that his grandmother kept interrupting by making the silence tremble, he hated Alda for taking him away from his mother

—Let me hold the little fellow for a while

followed by a woman's name he'd forgotten, what was she called, if at least he could find the same lacy comfort in his hospital bed, the father of the stain on the shoe

—I would advise you to think long and hard before carrying off that pearl

whereas his own father never belittled him, he merely avoided him, except when they were up in the hills, he would fetch the tennis balls for his father, who received them not in his hand but on his racket

—Put them there

like a tray made of strings onto which he unenthusiastically dropped the balls, the owner of the haberdashery shop continued to intrigue him

—Who exactly are you?

and the man didn't respond, so many mysteries and the combination of those mysteries and the pain was making him feel rather dazed, perhaps death meant living in another way, given that the dead were so active in the house, at certain moments he stopped existing and was aware that he had stopped existing until his heart and his liver sprang into life again on the screens, and if they were to attach fuses to his gray matter all his thoughts would be revealed

—Letting your mind wander helps

he opened the door where the flowers mingled with the bushes and the weeds in the overturned flowerpots, he tried the bell on the porch door, but the clapper was missing, he knocked, not a sound, he wiped the glass with his sleeve, he thought he could see Dona Irene and then finally a pedestal table with no vase on top and then him on his mother's lap, his cheek pressed against her lace bodice, now surfacing, now wrapped in a cocoon where, if he had his way, he would live eternally, don't pick me up

—Let me hold the little fellow for a while

walking over to the well and the pump with the broken handle, a reflected face, which it took him a while to realize belonged to him, then the owner of the haberdashery shop

—How you've changed, my friend

and he hadn't changed, it was the well that was wrong, when he reached the age when he was taller than his father all the rackets were left in a corner and all the tennis balls lost, and since the bushes had grown it was impossible to find them, as impossible as it was to find the Englishmen's hotel or the entrance to the mine, his father would no longer whisper to him

—You know

he intertwined his fingers so tightly he couldn't separate them, untangle them, his mother

—Now you've done it

freeing an index finger, a little finger, part of his thumb, the source of the Mondego in the same spot unless the mountain people had moved it, he found a goat looking at him, eyelids drooping, rolling thoughts slowly around in its mouth, and when he saw the goat the pain eased, he returned to the well and his features were stuck to his cheeks but upside down, the stain on the shoe

—Don't worry, death will sort everything out

as if death existed, and it doesn't, there he was on his mother's lap, and a battered iron cradle waiting in the cellar, his mother opened his father's letter and inside was a small carnation that scattered its dry petals on the floor, the prose written out neatly after several attempts, and she found the writing hard to decipher because of all the inkblots, pressing down too hard on the pen nib and putting too much glue on the envelope, his father's hands free again and him studying them fearfully, he bent his ring finger and his little finger and the fact that they obeyed proved nothing, they must be his, unless someone had screwed on some new ones, he could feel the lace and his mother's neck on the hospital pillow, despite the pleat she'd put in the dress the stain was still there, his grandmother

—There seems to be a stain

her glasses glued to it

—Perhaps a bit of benzene

even if you don't believe me, and you clearly don't, well, we haven't seen each other for years, I spent tonight with you, Maria Otília, me in the middle of the bed where the nurses put me and me hoping you would touch me and you on the very edge of the mattress hoping I wouldn't touch you, and I didn't touch you, so that you wouldn't repel me with an exasperated elbow

—Can't you sleep?

one leg sticking out from under the sheet, and since the blind wasn't down I felt very moved by the sight of that foot, tempted to pick it up in my cupped hand, kiss it, the foot escaping

—Shall I go and sleep in the living room?

and my palm empty, apart from my nose and my pursed lips, wanting, wanting you to forgive me, that would be best, because I love you, I would promise to fold the towel neatly and then forget, just as I would promise to turn off the faucets properly and not leave magazines on the floor, and then

I remembered the trains and I smiled, there has to be something in life to make me smile, perhaps I could smile at the pain, I'm not sure, despite the nurse saying

—His face is a blank

what if he were to ask the owner of the haberdashery shop

—Who exactly are you?

the man silently making himself comfortable on the balcony and the suspicion that in the silence

—I would be you if you were still alive

going back to a house where his grandfather no longer leafed through the newspaper, after his wife died the pharmacist wouldn't serve anyone, whereas with me, not even the pain weighed on me, so excited was I by the outlines of the swallows and the April clouds moving horizontally along the wires, if I'd had a son I would go looking for the source of the Mondego with him, I might whisper

—You know

and I wouldn't need to say anything more because my son would know just as the child I was knew, a baby frog hopped onto my boot and lingered for a moment, throat pulsing, look at the sparrows in the chestnut trees, look at the morning light on the ivy, the bells ringing out for the Elevation of the Host, and my grandmother sticking out her tongue, which I had never imagined to be so long, to receive the Host from the priest and receive it with as much pleasure as a lizard swallowing a fly, the smell of benzene filled the living room and the stain was still there, not a burn mark or grease, so what was it, my mother giving up with the benzene

—What kind of stain is it, then?

my grandmother returning to our pew with the fly in her mouth and the ecstatic look of a saint on the altar, ready to ascend into Heaven surrounded by jars of jam and wooden spoons, holding one of those spoons out to me

—Do you want to take Communion, Antoninho?

not a wafer or a fly, syrup and fruit, the pill was making him choke and while he was choking, nails, tacks, hooks, the stain on the shoe

—The edema is increasing in his lungs, I just hope that we

and he wasn't interested in what he went on to say, he was interested in the bare foot sticking out from under the sheet, when his father died he didn't show his grief, he sat under the elm trees smiling at the trains, the one o'clock fast train, the eleven o'clock freight train, the four o'clock mail train bringing the newspaper and the letters from the emigrants to France, he was sorry that the little frog didn't hop from his boot to his father's but instead vanished in among the mosses, a clown who tripped on a stone and clung to a tree trunk and Clotilde

—Oh, what a clown, how awful

and his mother outwardly agreeing

—Awful

and inwardly intrigued, she put the carnation in the little box where she kept her bracelets and that she would open now and then, feeling happy, the second letter contained a clover that as luck would have it didn't have four leaves, in the third a copper ring on which two hearts intertwined, Júlia

—He must have bought that cheap at the market

and his mother saying nothing, keeping quiet, smiling like him at the trains, when she swallowed the Host his grandmother was a person again, not a lizard, the taste of the jam would stay on his gums for hours and made him feel as if he were still eating it, he sucked at his gums, savoring the taste, and found himself in the kitchen again, and in the kitchen he found the tub where they used to bathe him, and going upstairs he found the other rooms in the house, the bedrooms, the study, the balcony and the family in the living room, his mother wearing her cheap copper ring, his grandfather folding up the newspaper, his uncle not in Spain and his grandmother holding the tea strainer, outside, the chickens settling down in the chicken run, where there was a shape larger than the birds that were not on the perches but pecking about among the flaking plaster, the earth and the grit, a shape to which his grandmother was calling

—Antoninho

then forgetting all about him down below surrounded by screens.

4 April 2007

Now yes, finally, yes now, dozens of swallows at the hospital window, no rain, the chestnut tree intact and Senhor Casimiro sitting by his bed offering him the jar of candy

—Would you like one, my dear?

everything in order then, he looked for the pain and it wasn't there, he could move his arms if he wanted, sit up in bed, leave, the nurse unplugged the screens, removed the IV drip, turned off the oxygen, and the swallows still ceaselessly there outside the window assuring him

—You don't have to pay a cent, we came gratis

his grandmother adding potatoes to the fish, cabbage, carrots, saying as she always did on the subject of carrots

—They put a sparkle in your eyes

and as always he would blink and his eyes felt just the same, he was certain that Maria Otília was there, not on the edge of the bed but close by

—I'm not bothered about the towels anymore

other people around too, Dona Lucrécia, Dona Irene, the pharmacist putting his tongue away in the purse of his mouth

—As strong as a horse, he'll live to be at least a hundred

a horse that wouldn't be led up into the mountains, he lingered in the meadow, but why, when his legs could run through the pine forest, the stain on the shoe let go of his wrist

—He's lasted longer than I expected

the father of the stain on the shoe adding

—You can't even get dying right

not in the hospital ward, of course, but in the village, he tried to remember how old he was, although what did it matter if the pharmacist had promised him he would live to be a hundred, the blonde foreigner at the Englishmen's hotel sitting on the edge of the swimming pool and soon the tungsten miners would be back, perhaps his mother would buy him some new boots next week and the maid would grease them, she would leave them out on the step until the smell had gone, his mother would put cotton wool in the toes of the boots until he grew into them, Clotilde not picking him up because his boots stank

—He must weigh a ton

and I must weigh a ton, Dona Clotilde, my mother says I'm made of lead, it intrigued him that the illness was growing inside the lead and yet he felt neither surprise nor terror, the ivy was growing taller on the wire frame, everything was trembling, breathing, boiling, including the old ladies eager to bury him in their shawls, how would he defend himself if one of them were to bite him or if a stray dog were to crouch down with him between its paws, where is this breeze coming from and this sort of cold, the man who produced coins from his nose

—I'm not going to earn any money from you guys

stormed off, his grandmother pointing with her fork at the fish on his plate

—Why don't you start eating, what are you waiting for?

and what was he waiting for, if one of the screens remained on, not a word and yet there were so many words
inside him, the source of the Mondego continuing to come
and go, he wanted to keep it there while he waited for a little
frog to choose him, he lay down on the rock until he could
feel all the things around him breathing and imagine they
were somehow his companions, his grandmother's fork

—Talking and eating is bad for the digestion

his stomach is beginning to hear and it isn't working, it
stops, wakes up halfway through the night, even though the
nights are over, after some difficult dreams, where did his
grandfather's gaze end if it didn't stop at the newspaper or
the trees, the stain on the shoe to his mother

—With today's treatments the end of life is usually very
peaceful

but he didn't hear, distracted by Senhor Liberto dispatch-
ing the trains, as well as the flag, he had a cornet hanging
from a strap round his neck, he realized that the swallows
were not today's swallows but from a previous April, he worried about their droppings now that they were dressing him
and not in clothes from the little cupboard in his room but
in a suit brought from home and a tie that they took time
to line up on his chest, his mother parted his hair and his
grandmother

—All dressed up like that, you look like a grown man

his father was waiting for the tennis ball, which, for the
first time, he couldn't find, he looked under this bush, then
that, in a hole where he thought a snake might be, and despite the snake there he was on hands and knees, creasing
the suit they had brought from home while his grandmother
ordered the maid to heat up the water for the tub

—After all, it's your wake, Antoninho, what will people think?

he could hear the miners' pickaxes and now and then see the lights on their helmets in between the mimosas, Júlia holding the copper ring

—You mean you're going to marry the clown?

his tie got caught on a branch and tore when he pulled it free, despite the frenzied buzzing of the wasps he heard the fabric tear, after his stroke his father with a blanket over his knees and one hand paralyzed, they gave him milk to drink through a tube and his useless hand was so thin, with the other he reached out to take the ball he couldn't find, when he woke there was his father in the dark, silhouetted against the mountains, once he said

—Dad

his hand imagining he had found the ball but there was no ball, I'll get it, just wait, perhaps the ball of the illness in his intestines that the stain on the shoe showed him on the X-ray

—See this here?

and why didn't they just take it out, the way the man did who produced coins from his nose, no tickling, no pain, him at the Englishmen's hotel

—Here's your ball, Dad

no

—Daddy

man to man because he no longer needed cotton wool in the toes of his shoes

—Here's your ball, Dad

indifferent to his mother's complaints

—Soon there won't be boots big enough for you

she didn't put him on her lap, he found no lace into which he could dissolve who he was and forget himself, he tried to return to a lost happiness and the fact that he belonged solely to himself terrified him, who would protect him from the world, I'm not this person, I'm the schoolboy who was always outdone by the fat kid who knew all the rivers, the boy who used to eat unripe fruit and collect insects in a matchbox, his grandmother pushing his food together on his plate

—Don't spread the fish around on your plate to make it look like you've eaten it

just as he used to put little seeds in the matchbox to feed the insects, if the stain on the shoe were to tie his good-luck ribbon around his wrist he might, just might, who knows, who could deny it, get better, Dona Irene stroking his head

—He fell asleep like a little saint

and then day would come and him alone in his room, shivering even though he was wearing his pajamas, the chestnut tree white, the sounds in the house very shrill, this wasn't where he belonged, he belonged to a warm neck and an arm keeping him from slipping down onto the floor, the spring lasted at most a few minutes, then came to an end, Senhor Liberto on the deserted platform

—Trains?

they changed the village station, leaving his grandfather with no newspaper, the blonde foreigner put all her creams in a basket, every vertebra standing out clearly down her back like the beads on his mother's necklace, forming not a circle but a straight line, the hotel owner, with no customers, locked the door and came down the steps, all that remained was the piano tuner in the bus, but there were no sparrows and no elms, a rook in a eucalyptus tree thinking, and Maria Otília when they told her about him

—Oh really?

her dyed hair making her face look harder and a certain difficulty in bending down, what happened to the foot sticking out from under the sheet and the murmurings on the telephone interrupted by infuriated tapping on the mouthpiece

—Would you mind not spying on me?

and him between the bedroom and the living room, the murmurings growing louder

—The fool just can't get it into his thick head that I can't take any more

none of which would be of any importance if his mother

—Antoninho

and her breast the place where he could anchor his fear of the world, he closed his eyes and saw eucalyptuses, ash trees, not just the closed door of the hotel, all the windows boarded up, the box hedges in the garden and the swimming pool still there, he scoured the lawn for any trace of the blonde foreigner, but no sign of footsteps, Senhor Liberto took off his cornet and put down his flag and stood motionless beneath the cawing of the crows, tell me, Senhor Liberto, how can you breathe without trains, how get through the days, his wife brought him turnip greens and he didn't even look at the pan, trying to discover where the railcars were now, he lived in a little house beside the station, where he would sit and listen to the breathing of the mountains in the hope that it might become the breathing of a locomotive gone astray, his wife

—Liberto

and Senhor Liberto loading his rifle

—Damn those crows

resting the butt on the ground, removing his shoes, placing his chin on the mouth of the barrel, pressing the trigger with his toe, and it took them a hell of a long time to put him together again

—There's an ear missing, isn't there?

he remembered the dented cornet lying among the railroad ties and his grandmother

—He must have had big lungs to blow on that thing

speaking of cornets, there were the Klaxon calls of the wild ducks flying off in search of the lake, one afternoon he and his father at the source of the Mondego found a female duck that couldn't fly and that hopped out of their way, and the following week there was no wild duck, just a few feathers and a bloodstain turning pink in the water, then no feathers and no blood, just the rocks and the mud, his father came over to him, he thought he was about to touch him, but he drew back, he probably found him as repellent as Maria Otília did, although why he didn't know, his grandmother pointing at the fish with her knife

—It's wrong not to eat all your food when there are so many poor people going hungry

half of Senhor Liberto in the cemetery, the other half pricking the curiosity of the dogs, some thrushes in the wild fig tree staring at him, now with one eye, now with the other, a beetle beating against the back of his neck, unable to escape, and those long-legged insects that walk on the surface of ponds, the stain on the shoe

—He's finally at peace

panicking over some remark by his father and how could

he be at peace when there were dozens of swallows at the window, his mother

—When I was young that bird broke one of its legs

which Júlia treated by using a bit of reed as a splint and feeding the bird with seeds, Alda wasn't brave enough to pick it up

—You can't imagine how ugly swallows are close up

so much hope in April and then nothing but a seething mass of critters, he missed the pain he had lost, he didn't know the names of the rivers when he was at school, Maria Otília left him and his father wouldn't touch him, the garbage truck will take me away before the first cars and the market trucks appear, along with more wretches like him, take him to the outskirts of Lisbon, where they will turn him into dust that will dissolve in the rain, what if he were to run toward the vineyard and the crows didn't denounce him

—He went thataway

he might manage to escape, his grandmother filling his trouser pockets

—Take some bread, dear

he looked for his bicycle in the storeroom but the chain was broken, I can't do figure eights around the chestnut tree, I'm sorry, Uncle, don't get me wrong, his grandmother saying when he opened the gate

—Congratulations

a pine forest, another pine forest, he used to hear the goats with the goatherd walking behind them in silence, why are country people so silent, even in the café on a Sunday, and he couldn't tell them apart, the goatherd and Virgílio or the man who took care of the orchard, pulling up the slow-growing weeds, now and then you heard a kind of struggle and the following day something was lying prone in a ditch with a hoe or a rake in its back, then along came the cortege and after the cortege and the bells the usual silence, he never overheard a conversation, an argument or someone crying, cackling laughter like rooks and sobbing like turkeys, he fell ill the way animals do, uncomplaining, the stain on the shoe

—If he'd come to see me six months ago

but then why would he have come six months ago when he was strong as a horse and sure to live until he was at least a hundred, him as a little boy watching the snow and the weightless universe outside, houses afloat, the church adrift, his mother wielding a broom and with a scarf on her head

—Do you want to be late for school?

and now she can't even remember her husband, she remembered a clown clutching a tree trunk and a woman saying

—What an awful idea

about what precisely she didn't know, what was so awful, not knowing frightened her, what's happening to me, I had this son, I had others or perhaps no son at all, sometimes I had a son and sometimes I didn't

—A son, what an idea

the woman who had been at the birth with a bowl and some towels, two towels folded up and bearing the initials of his grandfather's grandfather, one made of linen, to wrap the baby in, and another not made of linen, to soak up the blood, the woman who attended the birth was Jacinta, the same age as his uncle but born in August

—When I tell you to, push hard

and she didn't know what that *awful* meant nor if she'd

had more sons, the mother of Dona Jacinta Maria do Socorro, the brother who worked as a frontier guard, Fernando, his mother

—Fernando Albino Pereira

falling silent because of the pain and pushing hard, obedient, one or two paths unblocking in her memory among hundreds of closed-off paths, bringing fragments she couldn't put together, Clotilde Araújo Silva, Júlia Sarmento Pires, Alda Roma Gonçalves, the curate's first housekeeper having an attack, thrashing around near the trellis, and the curate, who was only young then, sprinkling her with holy water

—Begone, Satan

the woman attending the birth placed the palm of her hand on her belly

—Only push when I say so, all right?

and the curate's housekeeper still writhing around, foaming at the mouth, the pharmacist had the devil of a job to put some drops on her tongue, his mother

—When I said *a son, what an idea,* what was I trying to say?

and the absence of memory made her shrink back with anxiety, her voice suddenly filled with astonishing energy

—Seven pounds and two ounces

but seven pounds and two ounces of what, given that the what belonged to a blocked channel, he wanted to sleep and for his body to empty itself of whatever else was in it, duodenum, pituitary gland, Bellini's ducts, his mother holding a broom and with a scarf on her head

—Do you want to be late for school?

his grandfather's cough heading for the living room, beneath the cough his slippers and between the cough and the slippers a void, furniture full of musty clothing and hats and magazines, one day when he opens the chest his mother's breath will be there among the breath of the deceased

—Who are you?

and so he would immediately slam it shut to avoid questions, seven pounds and two ounces wrapped in a linen towel and now off for a stroll down the alleyways while the crows plunge into the cornfields, the curate's first housekeeper was walking on water in the city hospice, preaching to the Philistines, when his father died he felt like putting a little frog in his pocket to remind him of the suffering of the rocks

—When I tell you to, push hard

seven pounds and two ounces that they wrapped in linen, and him setting off down the rivers toward the sea, he was wrong about the swallows, because the rain continued to fall, he was wrong about the trains but not about the rivers, almost every day his grandmother would turn up at recess with a little bag of nuts and apples and he was always afraid his classmates would call him a baby

—Why don't you start eating, what are you waiting for?

he wasn't waiting for anything, only for his grandmother to leave so that he could hurl the bag against the wall, shouting

—Soppy old woman

he was perfectly capable of driving the cart, not just down the bramble-lined path but into the main square, if Virgílio would let him, he suddenly remembered the surprise and terror he had felt in the hospital and said self-mockingly

—Easy as pie

for we imagine how things will be before they actually happen and then they turn out to be just that, easy as pie, the woman who attended the birth held him upside down and slapped his bottom

—He'll breathe, don't worry

seven pounds and two ounces of secretions and folds of skin and a purple cord attached to his belly button, if his mother licked him the way sheep do and covered him with her belly to protect him from illness instead of touching him with hesitant fingers

—Who are you?

his father with a blanket over his knees, searching for two words

—You know

among the half a dozen words at his disposal, no, not half a dozen, two or three, no, not two or three, none, bubbles of spit that burst silently, it wasn't only the peasants who didn't speak, hundreds of times Maria Otília had said

—Has the cat got your tongue?

he felt like answering back but there were too many emotions wanting to be expressed, when he reached the balcony he couldn't see the buildings opposite, he could see the outline of the mountains, he couldn't pay attention to Maria Otília because of the difficult figure eights he was doing, his uncle running toward him hoping to grab the saddle and divert him

—You'll end up in the flower bed

with a row of bricks protecting the narcissi, the house belonged to his grandmother's father, who, accompanied by a friend wearing gaiters, would wander through the rooms after supper showing him the tables and the bronzes

—All this is mine, Adelino

his grandmother forgetting her fish

—What do you mean *all yours?*

and his grandmother's father apologizing

—Just a manner of speaking, my child, forgive me

disappearing into the china cabinet, no swallow at the window, no rain either, just the windowpanes and beyond them no clouds, no sky, as he left the village he passed the bus where the piano tuner was still sitting in his seat

—We're alone, aren't we?

not waiting, no one was waiting now, not even the barefoot child

—Bread, bread

standing next to an ash tree, and even the mountains absent, a bird heading off toward the dam, no, not a bird, the idea of a bird, had he been in the hospital or was the hospital just an invention like everything else, the stain on the shoe

—Good-bye

and he wanted to feel sorry, but sorry for whom, who wants to see the beautiful boat, etc., etc., yes, sir, you're right, we're alone, when he looked again, the piano tuner had vanished, Maria Otília distracted

—Oh really?

and so just as when the hotel owner bolted the door and came down the steps, when he bolted the door and came down the steps there was no door, no steps, explain that to me while I'm still capable of hearing, for I can hardly hear anything, what actually happened, don't say

—You know

and don't sit down next to me to see what isn't there, help me until there's no need to help, a person scolding him

—Do you want to be late for school?

without his grandfather's cough, and beneath the empty cough, just one person

—Do you want to be late for school?

and then the surprise and the terror came back to bid him farewell, there were some boards missing on the station platform, repeat *come and see the beautiful boat,* were those the right words, he imagined they were, he imagined they weren't, that beautiful boat was quite frankly improbable, a different verse but which one, patching up the platform with planks from the dismantled counter and bits of newspaper left in a corner, he found his uncle's suitcase lying open in the middle of the newspapers, the suit they'd dressed him in too tight in the shoulders, some defect in the trousers hurting his legs, what became of the pain, what became of the illness

—We've done what we can, now we just have to wait

in the midst of the vague shapes, vague lights, echoes where there should be no echoes, a lock of his mother's hair escaped from beneath her scarf, how did you become blind, Mom, unable to see me

—Who are you?

and suddenly the sea began to rise in his head, flooding the sewers, covering the rocks, shrinking the beach, this was at the start of the love affair or the marriage, how am I supposed to remember, I remember a lilac blouse, that we came by bus and the bathers put up sunshades, Maria Otília still telling him off at the time, grabbing his arm and saying

—Do you want to be late for school?

was it Maria Otília or his mother, he thought it was probably his mother, don't make me work too hard, no, not my mother, it must have been Maria Otília

—Do you want to be late for school?

tiny steps, his little shoulders hunched, his gums that

can still taste a remote lunch, covering the mouthpiece of the phone with one hand

—Would you mind letting me speak freely?

or not even a lunch, faded memories

—Your father

come and see the beautiful boat about to put to sea and there is the sea and them leaving their robes, their sandals and the bag full of knickknacks in a spot where they thought the waves wouldn't reach, except that they did, the way she had of picking up the objects, piling them up, running, the mind has these manias, when you're least expecting it such clear images, Our Lady is in the boat, and this was almost certainly true, the angels will row, the fat boy of the fourteen rivers, him with no rivers at all saying to the stain on the shoe, concealing his pain

—I'm fine

in the hope that if he concealed his pain he would get better, and he did, him saying to Maria Otília

—What about my father?

and his mother's gums paused to think, biting down hard on the beautiful boat, then thinking again, the stain on the shoe

—He's lasted longer than I expected

biting down harder and a tendon in his neck, lasting longer, moving the robes, the sandals and the bag full of knickknacks, not moving the swallows, because it was still winter

—It doesn't matter, forget it

it doesn't matter if the sea carries us off, forget it, what did we do down here, a clown embracing a tree trunk, no, a boy on a bicycle colliding with a granite pillar and the boy a clown, diapers, a catheter, a tube up his nose, nice boys don't spill their medicine or play with their food, they behave sensibly, so take this pill, Senhor Antunes, I don't want to see a single stain on the napkin, not bad so far, go on, if necessary we can bring a bowl and two neatly folded towels, not just thrown down on the floor, towels bearing the initials of his grandfather's grandfather, a linen one to wrap him in and another for the blood he doesn't have, if only I could find a vein but I can't, not a drop of blood, we need to disinfect this room, remove the equipment, change the mattress, a new patient today, and a younger one, poor thing, not the intestines this time, the lungs, it makes you wonder if God exists and if he does exist if he simply doesn't care, after my shift I'll go see a movie or pay for sex with some woman, it doesn't matter, the gurney has axles like a cart, where did that memory come from, on a bramble-lined path, and why brambles, it's as if Senhor Antunes, already wearing the suit his family brought in a paper bag, were waiting for something or other or ready to give something or other to a person I can't see, a tennis ball, for example, what a foolish image, offering a tennis ball to some Tom, Dick or Harry who isn't even looking at him, Maria Otília, and such a strange Maria Otília, if you'd come to see me six months ago, I doubt there'll be any swallows this year, the hospital budget doesn't run to birds, perhaps crows or rooks in a village up in the mountains, men selling boots at a provincial fair, a woman bending over a jewelry counter and Senhor Antunes by the rivers heading down to the sea, Maria Otília with her dyed hair

—Oh really?

meanwhile, instead of falling asleep on her lap, his cheek

pressed against the lace of her bodice, he was sitting on the floor as his mother was setting up the sewing machine, then he curled up at her feet to listen to her sing.

EXEUNT OMNES

(2009, 2010)

ANTÓNIO LOBO ANTUNES, born in Lisbon in 1942, trained as a psychiatrist and was called up as a military doctor in Portugal's doomed colonial war in Angola, an experience that marked much of his writing. Lobo Antunes's first novel, *Memória de Elefante* (*Elephant Memory*), appeared in 1979, and he has since published nearly thirty more, as well as several collections of his *crônicas* (a selection of which is available in English as *The Fat Man and Infinity & Other Writings*). His work has brought him many literary awards, including the prestigious Prémio Camões and, most recently, the Premio Internazionale Bottari Lattes Grinzane. He is one of Portugal's foremost contemporary writers.

MARGARET JULL COSTA has translated the works of many Spanish and Portuguese writers, among them the novelists Javier Marías, José Saramago, António Lobo Antunes, and Eça de Queiroz and the poets Fernando Pessoa, Sophia de Mello Breyner Andresen, Mário de Sá-Carneiro, and Ana Luísa Amaral.